'Thorne has delivered a gem' *Esquire*

'A masterpiece of menace and unease . . . You'll read it in one jaw-dropping sitting. *Cherry* is that rare thing, a perfect novel' *Zembla*

'More Calvino or Schnitzler (and think here of *Dream Story*, filmed by Kubrick as *Eyes Wide Shut*) than Kafka in its subtle transformations and deceptions . . . Reading *Cherry* is like looking at a photograph of an everyday scene or identifiable face taken slightly out of focus. Everything in the picture may be recognisable, but at the same time that slight loss of perfect definition renders everything altered or suspect or "wrong". It is that distance that gives this novel its strength'
Robert Edric, *Spectator*

'*Weird Science* meets *American Psycho* . . . taut and considered' *Time Out*

'Compulsively readable, intelligent and satirical . . . his quirkily poignant sixth novel explores the loss of innocence and idealism which provokes a desperate need for fantasy and illusion . . . *Cherry* is a requiem for lost idealism and it deserves high praise'
The List

'At the heart of this slice of reality lies a mystery that turns it into something more complex, and more satisfying'
Financial Times

'A mixture of noirish thriller and Borgesian fantasy'
New Statesman

'Gripping'   *S*

D1103209

Matt Thorne was born in 1974. He is the author of *Tourist* (1998), *Eight Minutes Idle* (winner of an Encore Prize, 1999), *Dreaming of Strangers* (2000), *Pictures of You* (2001) and *Child Star* (2003). He also co-edited the anthology *All Hail the New Puritans* (2000) and in 2004 published his first children's book, *39 Castles 1: Greengrove Castle* (2004).

CHERRY

A NOVEL

MATT THORNE

PHOENIX

A PHOENIX PAPERBACK

First published in Great Britain in 2004
by Weidenfeld & Nicolson
This paperback edition published in 2005
by Phoenix,
an imprint of Orion Books Ltd,
Orion House, 5 Upper St Martin's Lane
London WC2H 9EA

1 3 5 7 9 10 8 6 4 2

A CIP catalogue record for this book
is available from the British Library.

ISBN 0 75381 914 7

Printed and bound in Great Britain by
Clays Ltd, St Ives plc

For Lesley

ACKNOWLEDGEMENTS

Richard Milner, Alan Samson, Mark Rusher, Susan Lamb, Emma Finnegan, Richard Thomas, Kirsty Dunseath, Katie White, Ian Claussen, Nicholas Guyatt, Borivoj Radakovic, Drazen Kokanovic, Ivo Caput, Alexandra Heminsley, Sarah Ballard, David, Kaye and Louise Thorne, Mark and Charlotte Sinclair and John Rush.

The author would also like to extend a special thanks to the proprietors of the Three Writers Losing Money bar in South Beach, Miami, in grateful appreciation of the free dinners, drinks and emotional support.

PART ONE

ONE

When all this started (2003), I lived alone in a dangerous borough of London. My postcode prevented me from doing most things; my credit rating took care of the rest. Unlike the other teachers at my comprehensive, I saw nothing virtuous in this. But I got a lot less hassle than the rest of the staff. The kids could sense my heart wasn't in it, and knew that, like them, I was just trying to get through the day.

Every couple of months, I was woken by screams. The screams always sounded the same and lasted for a maximum of two minutes. I had an alarm clock at the foot of my bed and when the screams woke me the time was always between three and three-thirty. The first time I heard a scream I went to the window and considered calling the police. But then I worried I'd become implicated in some terrible trial. So instead I simply wrote down the time of the scream and for the whole of the following week I looked for those yellow witness appeal signs, terrified I'd see one that said:

POLICE APPEAL – WITNESSES
At 3.24 am last night a young woman was raped and murdered and you could have stopped it but you didn't do anything you stupid selfish coward.

There were good people on the school's staff, but they ignored me. I understood why: there was something I conveyed which was desperately unhealthy. Not just the general malaise of an underachieving thirty-three-year-old man, but a deep soul-sickness I've suffered since I was six years old. I functioned well enough to have a place in society, but the self-destructive energy I emitted stopped me from accomplishing anything greater.

Still, every now and again someone dropped out of a dinner party at short notice and I got a half-hearted invitation. Social occasions scared me. Many people are surprised teachers are often shy, believing that because we can hold the attention of a thirty-student classroom or a hundred-strong assembly we have no fear of public speaking. But such people have no understanding of a school's dynamic. My students may start the day with the kind of drug cocktail that would distinguish a coroner's report, but all teens have fragile egos, and it's easy to keep them quiet if you know which buttons to push. In front of adults I fumbled anecdotes, forgot punch-lines and before long someone else always took command of the conversation.

I did have one colleague, Tom Carson, who occasionally invited me to dinner, but mainly as amusement for his wife Judith, a speech therapist. At first I was flattered by Judith's inordinate interest in everything I said. She insisted on sitting next to me, hung on my every mumble, and often asked me to go back and repeat certain key bits of information. Then one night she asked me if I'd ever had speech therapy and I realised her interest was professional. After that, she took to trying to fix me up with a succession of her friends. But it was always a disaster, and we never even reached the stage of swapping phone numbers.

This evening she'd invited a woman called Harriet who had recently abandoned a well-paid job as a nutritionist. I couldn't work out whether Judith had selected this woman as an ironic joke or because she genuinely believed I might benefit from having a healthy partner. As well as Harriet, there were a younger couple, Jake and Lauren, who'd been present at several of these past dinners and no doubt experienced great amusement at my romantic failures. Jake and Lauren were the kind of couple who were as enthusiastic about doing bad things to their bodies as they were about being healthy. Their own peculiar brand of holistic living included organic soda bread, wheatgrass juice and heroin; yoga, osteopathy and bareback orgies. They were fascinated by everything Harriet had to say and demanded to know what sort of training she would be going through.

'Well,' she said, 'what many people don't realise is that becoming a nutritionist is a bit like becoming an economist. Mathematics is as essential to the job as anything else.'

'Everything's maths, though, isn't it?' said Jake. 'When it comes down to it.'

'What about you two, though?' she asked. 'How did you meet?'

Jake put his arm around his wife's waist. 'I was going through a rough time. And I needed a nurse.'

Lauren smiled.

As usual, the dinner went on far too long and by the end of the evening I'd decided I had nothing in common with Harriet and felt eager to get away. I caught a night bus home and thought about what Jake had said. I couldn't believe that someone could decide what sort of woman they wanted and go out and find her. Lauren was the perfect nurse. Jake was a lucky man.

TWO

The last day of summer term was always stressful. Not the questions. Usually other teachers had grown bored of asking me why I wasn't going on holiday and steered clear, worried my sadness would make them feel guilty about their well-earned breaks. No, it was the unavoidable fact that I now had six empty weeks ahead of me, a realisation I managed to avoid confronting until the last possible minute.

Of course, there was more than enough paperwork and administration to fill the time and if I wanted I could use this period to become the most efficient teacher at the school, but I was unpopular enough without making everyone else look bad. Plus, I resented the idea of being alone at my desk while everyone else was sunbathing on a beach. So I usually spent the time lying on a sofa filled with a paralysing fear that stopped me doing anything more constructive than watching TV.

The last day was stressful for other reasons, too. I'm not the kind of disturbing pedagogue who gets freaked out by seeing his female students in the term's end outfit of stockings and suspenders that has somehow hardened into tradition even though few of these girls have heard of St Trinian's, but I couldn't help being unsettled by the impossible enthusiasm that filled the school. Most of my students had even less exciting summers to look forward to than I did, and those who had reached their final year would soon discover that the long-awaited world of work is a cruel disappointment, yet still they insisted on this fiesta. I got out of playing 'Twist and Shout' with the staff band by volunteering to monitor the peculiar kids who were frightened by their school becoming quite so exciting and preferred to sit in the library drawing pictures of petrol stations. After avoiding the after-school trip to the pub with the few students hairy enough to pass for eighteen, I headed home and beat my fists against the bed until I felt calm again.

Then, most years, I usually fell into a Friday night depression. This particular evening, however, I was struck with an irresistible urge to go out. This is extremely rare for me, and on the few occasions I did feel like leaving my flat I usually went into Central London, ate dinner in an Angus Steak House and watched a film on my own. But tonight, for some reason, I felt like drinking. More than that, I wanted to find a place where I'd be accepted. There are places for everyone, why not me? My neighbourhood, though poor, is particularly inclusive. Every time I walked home I saw Turkish men operating private members' clubs out of old newsagents, lively bars with discreet rainbows in their windows, and backstreet pubs where the 1970s were carefully preserved for anyone who couldn't cope with the last two decades. There were also, on the outskirts of my area, mysterious bars that glowed purple and black and looked like they'd been transplanted there directly from a dangerous dream. It was to one of these bars that I headed now. The one I chose had red curtains across the windows and was empty apart from the barmaid. I went in, took a seat at the bar and ordered a drink.

'Quiet tonight,' I said.

'Always is,' she replied. 'We cater for people who drink during the week. They're sacred of weekends.'

I nodded. 'You don't mind if I talk, do you?'

She shook her head. 'What do you want to talk about?'

'I don't know. Do you live in the area?'

'Yeah. My girlfriend and I have a place nearby.'

I nodded. She'd obviously said this deliberately, as a warning not to waste my time. I felt disappointed that she'd done something so obvious. I wasn't hungry for her, just decent conversation. I remained silent for a moment. The barmaid watched me as if my reaction to this statement would decide her on how she felt about me.

'Last day of school today,' I said quietly.

The barmaid laughed, as if I was making a joke. 'Best days of our lives.'

'No, I mean, I'm a teacher. Today was the last day.'

'Oh, I see. What do you teach?'

'English.'

'Really?' she replied, sounding interested. 'So does my girlfriend. She works at a convent school. If the nuns knew what she was really like, they'd kick her out.'

'Because she's gay?'

'No, there's plenty of that going on there, in a quiet sort of fashion. No, she's just, just . . .' She gave up and laughed in a helpless way. 'Pretty twisted.'

The barmaid seemed overcome with admiration for her perverted girlfriend. I kept quiet, wondering if she'd elaborate. But I couldn't help feeling jealous. It was like hearing an ex say she'd met the perfect man. It occurred to me that not only are there places for everyone, but also people. They're all out there, all these misfits and psychos, lurking behind deliberately worded personal ads or obsessively visiting a specialist website, and every single one has plenty of willing partners. I'd been single for nearly twelve years, but when I did date women at university it was never like that. Neither my girlfriends nor I felt safe voicing specifics, and all my sexual activity, no matter how successful it seemed, always ended with a sense of doomed disappointment.

The barmaid picked up a paperback. 'Have you read this?'

I looked at the cover. 'No . . . I don't actually like reading that much. Besides, I never have the time.'

She nodded and sat on a stool. Our conversation had come

8

to an end and she concentrated on her book, leaving me alone with my beer.

Ten minutes later, I finished my drink and got up to leave. As I did so, an elderly man came through the door, blocking my way.

'No, my friend, you're not leaving yet. Have another drink.'

I gave him my fiercest stare. But he smiled back. He wasn't a derelict, and his smart grey suit and neat hair made me prepared to give him ten minutes, rather than just pushing past. I had come here for acceptance, after all.

'OK. If you're paying.'

'Of course.'

The man put his arm around my shoulders and led me back to the bar. He ordered. Then gave the barmaid a CD.

'Track 8?' she asked.

'Very good. You've won yourself a drink.'

She replaced the pop music that had been playing with the old man's CD.

'Do you like the Chairman?' he asked.

I shrugged.

'You know he was buried with a packet of fags and a bottle of whisky? This isn't his best song, but it means the most to me. "It Was a Very Good Year".'

The three of us listened to Frank Sinatra singing about being seventeen. He was describing the girls of his adolescence, and the old man said, 'Frank Sinatra was seventeen in 1932, well, '33 really, as he was born in December. Would you like to guess how old I was in '33?'

'No.'

'Wise man. Three. I was seventeen in 1947. That was my very good year. Seventeen's a very good year for everyone, don't you agree?'

'Yeah. I suppose so. I mean, it was for me.'

'1947,' he said with a sigh. 'Do you know what's the worst thing about being alive?'

'That we have to die?'

He shook his head. 'No. I'm not a religious man, but it seems as stupid to believe that death is the end as it is to believe that it isn't. The worst thing about being alive is that you can't choose when you're born. You have to go on believing that being alive now at this present time is the greatest honour, and that the quality of life now is as good as it's ever been. Otherwise, you're seen as some kind of life-denying lunatic. Being a historian is just about acceptable, as long as you don't get too obsessed with the past. But this is just about the worst fucking time to be alive in the whole history of the universe.'

He had a point.

'In about sixty years' time they'll find a way to double or triple the human lifespan. That's within reach. Scientists will be able to lengthen telomeres and slow down ageing; plastic surgery will be part of our everyday life. Baldness will be a thing of the past and every adult will have perfect teeth. Thirty years ago, you could be content with your three score and ten. But to be alive now, even your age, is to strive for something you're never going to achieve. So you either say sod it and do whatever you want and accept your ridiculously impoverished situation, or you can do all the right things and hope your genes aren't going to fuck you in the arse. Maybe if you do all the right things from day one you'll get an extra decade or so, but I can tell you that every single person I've known who's switched to healthy living has died an early death.'

'The cockroach argument?'

'Yes, sir, that's right. Although let's make it rats as we're English.' He finished his whisky and ordered another. 'Anyway, all I'm saying is that it seems tough that I was seventeen in '47, instead of '57, or '67, or even '87.'

'I was seventeen in '87,' I told him.

He smiled. 'So you know what I mean. Was that perfect for you? Or would you have preferred to come of age in a different decade?'

'Actually,' I said, 'I have the opposite problem. My adolescence was so perfect that I wish it was still 1987. I'd like to live my whole life in 1987. People would grow older, but the fashions, music and culture would continue, even grow, but in exactly the same style.'

'Yes,' he said, 'you understand. Bring this man another drink.'

The barmaid put down her book and started filling a glass. She asked the old man, 'But isn't that how you feel about 1947?'

'No,' he replied, 'haven't you been listening? This is not how I feel about 1947. 1947 was a perfect year because I was seventeen. It was the time in my life that was wonderful, not the world around me. I'd grown up during the War, and while there were those who had more sex in those years than they did during the rest of their lives, I was too young to enjoy those kind of experiences. Girls my age wanted older men, and while I had a constant fear of death it wasn't sexy for me like it was for other people. So I was incredibly relieved when it all came to an end in '45, but it still took another couple of years before girls were interested in me. Most people would say '47 was a terrible year. We had the coldest winter for fifty years, old people were dying every day, and I'd just got a job in a factory. But the women, Jesus Christ, the women. The latest look was long, full skirts, more in America than England, of course, but we weren't far behind, and to me that's still the most erotic way a woman can dress. Strapless bras were also making their way across the Atlantic,' he chuckled, 'flying, I suppose . . . and there was this new vogue for bare shoulders.'

'In winter?' the barmaid asked.

'No, of course not in winter, but my girlfriend, Rose,

would dress up for me, in clothes I liked, when we were inside . . . God, I'll never forget that year.'

I don't know why I invited the old man back to my flat. I suppose it's because so much of what he said struck a chord in me, and I recognised his desires as an older version of my own.

And I had something I wanted to show him.

I poured him a tumbler of whisky from the bottle we'd bought on the way home, put on his CD, and sat him down in front of my television. Then I put on a video I had made during a few weeks in November 1987. 'Steve's Video No. 1'. My father, acting completely out of character, had bought me a video camera and I'd taken to the streets, shooting footage (from a distance) of every woman I found attractive. It might sound creepy, but I'm glad I did it. When I made the film it was a cure for loneliness, a shy man's hobby. I watched the tape a couple of times and found it boring. Ten years later I rediscovered the tape and the passage of time had made these images electrifying. Every single woman on that tape had become a hundred times more beautiful. Their absurd, alien outfits and outlandish hairstyles had become incredibly exciting. Usually I could only watch a few minutes of the video before being completely overcome. Tonight I watched the full hour. When it finished, I pressed 'stop' and turned round to see if it had worked on the old man. The small leathery semi-circles beneath his eyes glistened and when his gaze met mine he gave up any pretence of controlling his emotion and started sobbing with a terrifying intensity.

I knew exactly how he felt.

THREE

Usually I tried to avoid seeing my parents. My mother had me at fifteen and in spite of all the subsequent scandal somehow my birth and early childhood only strengthened my parents' relationship and they've stayed together for the last thirty-three years. Although they're now approaching their fifties, they refuse to act their age and these days lead a much more exciting life than me. That Saturday they were having a barbecue. I'd intended to avoid it, but to punish myself for the stupid night before I got up and went round to their house just before lunchtime.

The house was already full of people I didn't know. My age or younger, and relaxed in a way I could never be. My parents are intelligent, and although friends and family had assumed that having a baby so young would rob them of an essential part of their development, their commitment to each other had allowed them to simply postpone (and then endlessly extend) their last few years of youth. I felt like I was the adult, an angry neighbour who'd come over to tell them to turn the music down and somehow been sucked into the action. I didn't recognise anyone among the guests so I looked for my father. He was sitting by the giant chimney that took up a disproportionate part of the living room, turning it into two smaller square spaces with a narrow passageway between them. The house dated from the 1820s, and it was the closest thing my family had to a legacy. It had remained in my father's family since it was built, and my parents had lived here with my widowed grandfather until he died in 1987. Within two months of his death my mother had persuaded my father to begin a long process of renovation which cost the pair of them such a large percentage of their wages that it was almost as bad as having a mortgage. In my mother's defence, it has to be said that most of her renovations were designed to undo the damage that had been done to the property by my grandfather, an extremely perverse and whimsical man. An electrician by trade, he had plenty of contacts in the building world, and he used them to convert the previously light and airy house into a smuggler's den. He started by having thick black misshapen slate cemented into every wall, then added huge brass panelling and white netting at the windows throughout the house. His constant smoking provided the final yellowing that gave him the overall effect he craved. My mother persuaded my father to remove the slate and panelling, but when it came to her last, and greatest desire, she met with an iron resistance. There was no way my father was going to let her get rid of his chimney: it would, he told her, be like tearing the heart out of a human being.

My father sprang up and embraced me. 'Steve. We didn't expect you to show. Thanks so much for coming.'

'I didn't bring any food,' I told him. 'Or drink, for that matter.'

'Don't worry, we've got plenty.' He turned to the friend he was sitting with. 'Tim, this is my son.'

'Pleased to meet you. I'm the new neighbour.'

My father wandered off to get me a drink. I sat in his chair and asked Tim, 'When did you move in?'

'Two weeks ago. Me and my wife. She's not here today.'

I nodded, not really listening.

'She's at home,' he continued. 'She's in our bed. On her own, of course. Headaches.' He smiled. 'You understand.'

I got the impression Tim wanted something from me. He was staring at me with a slightly mad intensity. I didn't know how to answer so I nodded twice, which seemed to reassure him. Tim was dressed more formally than anyone else at the barbecue party, wearing a neatly pressed blue blazer, a clean white shirt and a pair of black trousers. His brown hair was cut short, although even at that length there was the beginning of a curl. His face was extremely pale and his features were widely spaced out, making him look more like a child's toy than a grown man. He was drinking beer.

'Are you married?' he asked.

'No.'

'I met my wife when I was doing a postgraduate course in international relations.'

I nodded.

'She's Polish. My wife.'

'I see.'

'No one thought we'd ever get married. She used to abuse me in public all the time. Everyone else at the university started a campaign to split us up.'

My father returned with a beer for me. I got up from his chair.

'No, no,' he said, 'it's OK. You stay here with Tim. I've got to get the barbecue started.'

I could tell he wanted to get away from his neighbour. Well, there was no way he was going to leave me with him.

'Is Mum around? I was hoping to have a chat.'

'Mum? Yeah, I think she's in the garden. Do you want to come with me? Tim, you'll be all right on your own for a minute, won't you?'

Tim nodded. I followed my father out through the kitchen.

'Thanks a lot, Dad.'

'What?' he asked.

'Trying to abandon me with that strange man.'

My father laughed. 'Steve, I've been stuck with him for the last two hours. Besides, I'm sure this is only a temporary respite.'

I saw my mother sitting with some friends at the end of our

long garden. During the process of renovation she had done a deal to buy some land from one of Tim's predecessors, and the garden now extended down far behind our house.

'Steve,' she said as she saw me, 'I thought you weren't coming.'

'No, no, I said I'd make it if I could.'

She blew air through her lips. 'Yeah, but we all know what that means.'

Her friends laughed. I recognised one of them, a short brown-haired woman my mother called Squirrel. I couldn't remember her real name, even though I'd met her countless times before.

'I met your neighbour.'

They all laughed.

'Oh, he's all right,' said Squirrel defensively. 'He just seems strange. It's because he acts like he's been transported here from a different time.'

'What d'you mean?'

'He's just . . . so English.'

'The way he goes on about his wife all the time weirds me out,' another, younger, woman said. 'It's like she doesn't really exist.'

'Does he do that with everyone?' I asked.

My mother cooed at me. 'Oh, did Stevie think he was special?'

'Has anyone actually met her?' asked Squirrel.

'I have,' my mother replied. 'But only once . . . when they first moved in. She's very pretty.'

I'm certain my more serious emotional problems stem from my relationship with my mother. When I was about three or four, my father shot some Super-8 footage of the two of us together, and in the film you can see Mum play a series of simple tricks on me. Her playfulness borders on cruelty, and when I asked my father if she was like that all the time or just playing up to the camera, he had to admit that his parents had expressed concern about the way she behaved with me. It was obvious she loved me, but she treated me more like a doll or a pet or a funny toy than a baby. When I was a toddler she loved pulling my trousers down and giving me a playful smack on the bottom, and would mock the slow baby speed with which I did everything. My father found it disconcerting, but as it didn't seem to do me any harm he didn't intervene, preferring instead to balance things out by always treating me as a miniature adult. My mother's favourite trick was to say, 'Poor Stevie, poor Stevie,' when there was nothing wrong with me and then laugh when it induced tears and ask me what I was upset about.

Tim cornered me in the kitchen. I'd gone to the fridge for another beer to drink with my hot dog. He carried on talking as if our earlier conversation hadn't been interrupted.

'They didn't know, you see. She told everyone she was a virgin. I don't know why she did this, she still hasn't explained her reasoning to me. Maybe she was embarrassed, or thought people would judge her because she was Polish. But the truth is, she was completely different behind closed doors. In fact, the first time we slept together, she said to me, "Outside this room, I'm in charge, but when we're in bed you're the Master." I didn't take her seriously at first, I thought all she meant was that she was prepared to have sex with me. But that wasn't all she meant. She would do, or let me do, anything I wanted. Still does. And not in a submissive way, either. I mean, she submits to my will, but she's not like one of those boring horrible women who always wants to do it in the missionary position. She's just as happy to dominate me, if that's what I want.'

Tim was leaning in towards me as he spoke. I took a bite from my hot dog and had a swig of beer.

'It may not come as a surprise to you, Steve, but I'm not a very imaginative man. Certainly not when it comes to sex, anyway. I think it's because I'm such a serious romantic. I really am one of the most romantic people you'll ever meet. I don't just mean in the flowers and diamonds and champagne sense, although my wife gets all that as well, of course. I mean that I'm romantic in outlook. And there are some sexual acts, maybe you don't know what I'm talking about, but there are some acts which I find it impossible to equate with romance. Well, I used to, anyway, before my wife taught me how not to think that way. At first, because she wanted me to be the dominant, super-hetero male she let me run through my little list of fantasies, but in a ridiculously short space of time I had run out of ideas, Steve, I really had. That probably sounds pathetic to you. I had a woman willing to do anything, absolutely anything and my imagination failed me. You've never been in that situation, I can tell. The problem was, I think, that there are only a limited number of sexual acts that are exciting to everyone. And once you've done all these things a certain number of times, if you're going to . . . progress any further . . . it becomes a question of individual appetite. Lots of things that excite one person are completely ridiculous to someone else. So what we started doing, what she started doing, I should say, was writing little notes with ideas on them and the ones that worked for me as well as her were the ones we did. Although I have to admit that apart from a couple of ideas that seemed completely strange and abhorrent, almost everything she suggested seemed sexy to me, just because she'd suggested it. And while a couple of these things were hard to square with a con-ventional idea of romance, or the way a man should treat a woman, I found out that my fear that doing these sort of things together might distance you from a person was completely inaccurate. Sharing extremes brings people together. That probably sounds completely obvious to you, but it came as a real surprise to me, Steve, it really did. Do you understand?'

'I think so,' I told him. 'It sounds like your marriage is really strong.'

'It is, Steve, it is.'

I could tell he was waiting for a similar revelation from me, but all I could think to tell him was the way I'd felt at Tom Carson's house when Jake had said that thing about how he'd chosen his wife because he needed a nurse.

'That's exactly what my marriage is like, Steve. Exactly what it's like.'

'I'm really pleased for you, Tim. Shall we go join the others?'

He looked slightly deflated, but said, 'OK, Steve, yeah, let's do that.'

I don't know whether it was the presence of Tim or the desire to drink off my hangover that made me consume so much alcohol that afternoon, but I got so drunk that when my parents' house finally emptied at eleven, I suggested to Tim that the two of us should go somewhere else for a few more pints. My father was amazed to see me acting so out of character and asked, 'Are you sure you'll be able to find anywhere open at this time of night?'

'Yeah,' I replied, 'of course. The police are so scared of where I live that we make up our own licensing laws.'

'I don't want to go anywhere illegal,' Tim said nervously.

'I'm joking,' I told him, 'there's an ordinary pub a couple of streets away from me that stays open until three on the weekend.'

My parents realised that Tim was wavering and if he didn't go with me they might be stuck with him in their house for another hour. In order to prevent this, my father picked up the phone and said, 'I'll call you a taxi. They should be here almost immediately.'

My father came to the door when we left, waiting until he was certain Tim was safely in the cab. As drunk as I undoubtedly was, I could tell Tim was in an even worse state, and I opened both windows, hoping the cold air would stop him throwing up. I'd started to feel responsible for this peculiar man, and felt guilty about taking him away from his home and beloved wife.

'We don't have to go to the pub if you don't want to. I have half a bottle of whisky at my flat.'

Tim opened his eyes. He was slumped against the car door and I worried that if we went over a big enough bump it might spring open and fling him out. He reached for my jacket and said, 'A nightcap.'

'Exactly. We'll take it slowly. I'll make you a coffee and if you still feel rough you can sleep on my sofa.'

'Yes,' he replied, 'that sounds like the best idea.'

I changed my directions to the driver and we went straight to my flat. The driver didn't want to linger in my neighbourhood and as soon as we were on the pavement he snatched his payment and sped off. Tim followed me to my front door and waited while I slid a key into each of the three locks. My flat is on the third floor of a shared house and Tim was shocked by the appalling state of my hall and staircase. The landing's ceiling had recently fallen in and the floor was covered with thick white dust and chunks of plaster.

'Christ, Steve,' he mumbled as we came up the stairs, 'you should have a word with your landlord.'

'I should move is what I should do. But he's so desperate to get me out that he's leaving the place like this. Not that I care, I'm withholding the rent until he fixes the ceiling. Another two months and I'll have the deposit for somewhere decent.'

'Sharp thinking,' slurred Tim, steadying himself by grabbing hold of the banister. We went up the second set of stairs and I unlocked the door to my flat.

'Coffee first, then whisky?' I asked him.

He staggered inside and fell onto the sofa. I put the kettle on and went over to my stereo. I looked for something to play, then pressed the 'open' button next to the CD drawer. It slid open and I saw that the old man had forgotten his Frank

Sinatra CD. Oh well, it was suitable for the hour. I pressed the 'close' button, but the drawer remained open. I should have left it, but because I was drunk I used my thumbs to force it shut. There was an ominous clicking sound and when I pressed 'play' the stereo didn't register that there was a compact disc inside. I tried 'open' again, and when the drawer slid out I saw that the Frank Sinatra CD had risen over the rounded ridge of the plastic tray and there was only a quarter moon left visible.

'Shit.'

Tim roused himself. 'What's wrong?'

'I was trying to play a CD and I've fucked up my stereo.'

'Let me have a look,' he said. 'I'm brilliant at fixing technical things.'

I stood back. He came over and I explained the problem, and then left him while I went to pour the coffee. When I returned he'd managed to push the whole of the CD inside the machine, but was still insisting this wasn't a problem.

'There must have been something sticky on the rim of the CD,' Tim told me. 'But don't worry. Fetch me a Phillips screwdriver and I'll take the outer casing off, rescue the CD and get the stereo working again.'

'I don't have a Phillips screwdriver.'

Tim stared at me as if I was lying. 'You must have,' he said. 'How else can you fix your appliances?'

'I don't. When they break I throw them away and get new ones.'

'But that must cost a fortune.'

I shook my head. 'There's plenty of shops round here with a secret back room full of electrical equipment they'll sell you for next to nothing provided you pay in cash and don't mind carrying it home in a black plastic bag. The only reason I'm panicking is because that CD doesn't belong to me and it has a special sentimental attachment for the person who lent it to me and I don't know how easy it is to replace.'

'Who is it?'

'The CD? Frank Sinatra.'

'Well, that shouldn't be a problem.'

'Probably, but I'm worried it's a special, obscure edition. It definitely wasn't a "greatest hits".'

'You won't need to replace it. If you go and buy a Phillips screwdriver tomorrow all you need to do is take the casing off and you'll be able to slide the CD out with your fingers.'

I handed him his coffee. We stopped staring at the stereo and sat down.

'Tim, don't take this the wrong way, but can I ask you a question?'

He gave me a wary look. 'OK.'

'Why do you go on about your wife all the time? I think it really frightens people.'

He hadn't been expecting this. He stared at me in shock, then put his coffee down, bit his knuckle and stared at my wallpaper. I worried that he was about to start crying.

'I'm scared, Steve, really scared . . .'

'About what?'

'You're not married, you don't understand . . .'

'Understand what?'

'The worst thing about marriage.'

'Which is?'

'The fear.'

'What fear? That she isn't the one? That you might break up?'

'No, Steve, the fear that you'll stay together, but that you'll never . . . not completely . . . satisfy your wife.'

He sipped his coffee and waited for a reply. But I remained silent. How do you respond to a statement like that?

FOUR

I woke up at 8.45. I'd wanted a lie-in, but Tim was standing in my bedroom, trying to tell me something.

'Yes?' I asked.

'There's someone on the phone.'

'OK, Tim, tell them I'll be there in a minute.'

He backed out of my bedroom. I picked my clothes off the floor and put them on. Then I went into the lounge and took the receiver from Tim.

'Good morning, Steve, it's Harry Hollingsworth. I was at your flat the night before last.'

'I remember.'

'Well, the thing is, getting right to the point, I think I left my Frank Sinatra CD in your flat. I've got the case, but there's no actual CD inside. Can I come round and pick it up?'

'OK. But listen . . .'

'Great. All right, mate. I've got something I've got to take care of first, but I'll be round at eleven o'clock.'

He hung up. I turned round to Tim. My hangovers are never as bad as on the rare occasions when I've been drinking two or more nights in a row, but he must have been really suffering. He gave no sign of being in pain, although he did look shocked at still being here.

'Was that him?' he asked.

'Who?'

'The friend whose CD you borrowed.'

I grabbed a handful of his now grubby white shirt. 'You didn't say anything . . . ?'

'Of course not,' he replied, raising his hands in alarm.

'How did you know that was him, then?'

He shrugged. 'I didn't.'

I realised I was being irrational and let him go. He brushed his hair straight, then turned round and walked through to the toilet. He closed the door, but the walls were thin and I could hear him vomiting. When he returned he looked even paler than he had the night before. I offered him my telephone.

'Want to call your wife?'

He gave me a grateful smile. 'Thanks.'

I went through to the toilet to clean my teeth, shave and wash my face. I didn't usually like what I saw in the mirror, preferring to believe my mental image of how I looked, but today was particularly disheartening. My hairline hadn't quite reached the point where it was best to shave my head and be done with it (no matter how many nasty female journalists said this was the modern man's equivalent of a swoop-over, at a certain age it becomes the only viable option), but it was getting close. My stubble was almost entirely grey now, and my combination skin shiny in all the most prominent places and dull everywhere else. There was still something there to work with, but if I didn't change my lifestyle soon I'd be bidding farewell to the relatively reasonable looks of my youth after getting a pitiful amount of mileage out of them.

When I came back into the lounge, Tim was cooing endearments to his Polish wife. The moment he noticed me, he hung up.

'She's coming.'

'How does she know the address?'

He looked scared again. 'The letter on your table.'

'Oh,' I said, 'right . . .'

This started me wondering how Harry'd got my phone

number. Most teachers are ex-directory, unless they like getting crank calls from their female students. It was possible that I'd scrawled it down for him at the end of our drunken evening, but I had no recollection of doing so.

'OK,' I told Tim, 'don't leave until I get back, even if your wife arrives.'

'Why? Where are you going?'

'To get a screwdriver.'*

I put my shoes on and ran out the door.

* Don't worry, I do realise how pathetic this sounds. How could a thirty-three-year-old man grow up so inept that he doesn't even have a Phillips screwdriver in the house? But there are lots of men like me out there. In here. I meet them sometimes, men between twenty-four and thirty-five whose mothers thought that passing on traditional male skills was as dangerous as passing on old-fashioned attitudes if they were to achieve a new world order. For every mother who believed that teaching her daughter how to change a fuse was the first step to full equality, there was another who believed that her son might develop differently if denied this heritage. And I was more than happy to go along with this. In fact, I was so lazy that it suited me best not to have to do anything practical at all.

FIVE

I had no idea where I was going to buy a screwdriver. I headed towards one of the electrical equipment shops, then after about ten minutes I noticed a hardware store opposite the supermarket. I went in and bought the screwdriver, then returned to my house. Tim's wife had arrived and the two of them were huddled together on the sofa, as if I had kidnapped them. Tim's wife was as pretty as my mother had said she was, a slight woman with small, elegant features and dyed blonde hair. In order to defuse the tension, I marched straight over and offered my hand.

'Hi, my name's Steve, I'm your neighbour's son. Tim's told me a lot about you.'

'Brygida,' she offered shyly.

'Nice to meet you,' I replied, not attempting to repeat her name. 'Now, Tim, come and show me what to do.'

'It's really quite easy,' he told me.

'I'm sure it is. This is the right sort of screwdriver, isn't it? The man in the shop said it was.'

He nodded. The two of us went over to the stereo and Tim watched as I unscrewed the two screws on the left hand side of the metal casing.

'Do you want to make some coffee?' I asked Brygida. 'You'll find everything you need in the kitchen.'

Brygida seemed affronted by this suggestion, but I ignored her, moving round to the right side of the stereo. I undid the first screw. As I pulled it out the static charge made it dangle from the head of the screwdriver. I flicked it into Tim's hand and went to lift the metal casing.

'No, no,' he told me, 'there's eight more screws round the back.'

'How do you know that?'

'I had a look when you went out to buy the screwdriver. You're a very suspicious man, Steve.'

'I need to be. I spend all my time around children. What time is it?'

He looked at his watch. 'Nine-fifteen.'

'OK, this is fine, I should still be all right.'

'Why don't you turn the stereo round? That'll make it a lot easier.'

'But it'll get all tangled up in the speaker wires.'

'Detach the speakers.'

'See, I do need you here. Right, let's have a look at the back.' I unclicked the red and black catches that kept the left and right speaker wires in place and rotated the stereo so we could look at the back. Alongside the yellow and black label that said this was a *Luokan 1 Laserleite/Klass 1 Laserapparat* was a plastic sign with two triangles: one containing a lightning bolt, the other an exclamation mark. Between the triangles was the warning: CAUTION – RISK OF ELECTRIC SHOCK – DO NOT OPEN. I pointed this out to Tim.

'Why am I ignoring this warning?'

'If it's unplugged you won't get electrocuted.'

'Why doesn't it say that instead then? Risk of electric shock . . . if opened when still plugged in.'

I could hear the restraint in his voice as he said, 'I think they assume most people can work that out for themselves.'

The screws in the back were smaller than the ones in the side. I unscrewed them all and handed them to Tim.

'OK,' he said, 'now you should be able to lift off the casing.'

I tried to do this, but it wouldn't come free. For some reason, I had started to sweat heavily. I don't know why, usually I hardly sweat at all. I'd been panicking about the old man coming round, but it was OK, I had plenty of time. The stereo slipped out of my damp hands and Tim took it from me.

'I'll do it,' said Tim.

'Thanks. I'm just going to sit down for a moment. I think there's something wrong with my heart.'

'Your heart?' he said anxiously.

'Yeah, it's beating funny. My chest hurts. Let me sit down, I'm sure it'll pass.'

I pulled up a chair. Brygida brought us both cups of coffee. Then she retreated to the settee. Tim tugged at the casing and it came free. From where I was sitting all I could see was the two green circuit boards that ran down the left side of the stereo. I was impressed that something so ordinary, something smuggled into every home, could have a sci-fi image, the diodes, resistors, variable potentiometers, capacitors, power transistors and integrated circuits forming an aerial view of a twenty-fifth century cityscape. As my breathing returned to normal, I imagined myself living inside the giant black mansion that was really a slanted chip in the corner of the upper board, the tiny blobs of solder the cars of the employees who worked at my nearby chemical plant. If I could have chosen that life instead of my own, I would have made the swap in a heartbeat.

Tim dipped his hand inside the machine, rescuing the rest of the CD from the spindle table. There was a sudden snapping sound as he pulled it out from beneath the clamper.

'You stupid prick, you've snapped it.'

He lifted the CD from the machine and examined it. 'No I haven't, it's just a tiny chip in the enamel.'

'Well, that tiny chip's going to make the music sound like shit.'

'No it's not,' he protested, 'the information's not contained in that part of the CD. It won't make any difference.'

'Are you sure?'

'Of course I'm sure. Don't you know anything?'

I felt like hitting Tim, but restrained myself. He gave me the CD and I inspected the damage. It was only a small chip, but it was definitely visible. If I had the jewel case I wouldn't have worried, but as it was I couldn't help fretting that Harry might freak out.

Brygida asked, 'Can we go now?'

'Yeah,' I said, 'why don't you do that?'

After Tim and Brygida had gone, I sat down and stared at the CD. Would Harry notice? Unlikely. I was being paranoid. I'm not obsessive by nature, but this sort of thing always gets to me. Broken steroes, skipping CDs: they fill me with a horror most people would consider insane. It's not that I'm an audiophile, just that this feels like one of the few tasks I've been entrusted with that I ought to be able to manage. Every time a CD I own gets a scratch or starts to skip, I feel an immediate compulsion to replace it as quickly as possible. I don't really know why, and I don't think it counts as a librarian instinct as none of the CDs I own are especially obscure, and most are easily replaceable just by accessing Amazon, let alone eBay or some specialist site. It's not even the worry that if I don't replace the broken CDs someone will come to my house and want to listen to them, as I'm intensely anti-social and most of the music I own goes out of fashion three months after it's released. It just feels like failure not to be able to take care of this one simple thing. Books I couldn't give a toss about. I rarely read, so I hardly buy any and on the rare occasions I do find anything good I quickly pass it on to someone else in the staffroom so they don't realise what a terrible charlatan I am when it comes to my subject.

Harry arrived on time. I let him in and was about to hand the CD back, finger covering the chip, when he asked if he could come up.

I shrugged. 'OK.'

Noticing the chunks of plaster, Harry asked, 'Was this place like this last time?'

'Yeah, although my neighbours have kicked it around a bit since then.'

'Jesus, I was so drunk I didn't even notice. How can you live here?'

'It's OK,' I told him, 'I've got used to it.'

He considered this. 'Some men can get used to anything. It's a sign of mental strength. But it can also be a weakness. If you're happy living in squalor, how are you ever going to aspire to luxury?'

'I don't aspire to luxury.'

He laughed. We reached the top of the stairs. Harry rested for a moment, catching his breath as I opened the door. As we went inside he asked, 'Is there any of that whisky left?'

'A little. I had someone round last night and we drank most of it.'

'As long as there's enough for a glass. Or two glasses, if you'll join me.'

'I'll check. There should be.'

Harry sat down. I went out to the kitchen. There was more than enough whisky left so I poured two glasses. When I came back, Harry looked confused. 'Why did you dismantle your stereo?'

'Oh,' I said, 'it was a bet.'

Harry stared at me. I knew he was waiting for an explanation, but I kept quiet. He took the whisky from me, sipped it, and let out a deep sigh.

'So,' he said, rubbing his legs, 'I've got something to ask you.'

'OK.'

'I don't know how you're going to react to this, but I can promise you there's a very good reason for this request.'

'Which is?'

'The reason, or the request?'

'The request.'

'Ah, good, because I'm not going to tell you the reason. But the request is, can I borrow that video you showed me the other night?'

'Yeah, sure,' I said, handing it to him.

He grabbed my arm. 'This tape means the world to you, and yet you're willing to give it to me, a total stranger, without even extracting a promise when I'll return it.'

'Well,' I said, 'I would like it back.'

'Oh, don't worry, you'll get it back. Something good is going to happen to you very soon, Steve. You know what this tape is, don't you?'

'What?'

'It's a human scart plug, that's what it is. It's your scart plug.'

He finished his whisky and I asked him to leave, bored with his nonsense and no longer concerned about the chip in his Frank Sinatra CD, or about sacrificing my video to get this annoying old man out of my house.

PART TWO

SIX

A man can get himself into all sorts of trouble when he's home alone all day every day. Not reporting nocturnal screams was nothing compared to my failure to intervene in any of the manifold crimes I witnessed just going about my normal business in this neighbourhood. Weird stuff, too, like a gang of schoolchildren in skullcaps dismantling a parked car piece by piece. A woman telling me she'd just killed her baby and inviting me into her house to see the body when I said I didn't believe her. Strange men wandering up and down the street with toilet seats around their necks – although I suppose that's not a crime. My next-door neighbour Len, who curses with such elaborate imagination that it's impossible to visualise what he's talking about. I had no idea I got so many phone calls during the day. Market research, BT automata, cold callers. Foreign men asking to speak to people I've never heard of whom they swear usually answer this line. Do these people phone all the time or do they wait for the summer holidays? Voices from the taps. Men knocking at the door offering to tarmac my yard. Would I like to buy a carpet? Do I have money? His wife is pregnant and he's just broken down. It costs to get into the shelter and he's almost got enough. Do I want to change my central heating system? They're laying cable – would I like to take advantage of this once-only opportunity? Broadband internet access? Only £24.99 a month once you've paid the hidden £80 connection charge. It got so I was scared to open my door.

The last time I did, I found a smartly dressed Indian man standing on my doorstep. He was carrying a clipboard and I assumed he was going to ask me whether I was on the electoral roll. Instead, he said, 'Good afternoon, my name is Soumenda Jindal. I'm with YPW, can I come in?'

'You're with who?'

'YPW.'

'What's YPW?'

'I can explain, but will you let me in first? Don't worry, I'm not dangerous. Your friend Harry Hollingsworth sent me.'

I had to think for a moment. It had been a couple of weeks since Harry had been in my house and I'd all but forgotten the incident. But the man was so earnest that I decided to let him in.

'Are you having building work done?' he asked as we went upstairs.

'That's right,' I lied. 'Will this take long?'

'Well,' he said, 'that depends on you. I'm terribly sorry to ask this, but would it be at all possible for me to have a glass of water. This dust in the hallway, it's . . .'

'Of course,' I told him, 'go into the lounge and make yourself comfortable.'

Soumenda did as I instructed while I poured him a large glass of water from the tap. When I returned into the lounge he pointed at my dismantled stereo and said, 'You've cost me a fiver.'

'What?'

'Harry had a bet with me that you wouldn't have fixed that.'

'Oh,' I replied, pointing to the crappy ice-blue CX110 that the secret shop had sold me for a tenner. 'I bought a new one.'

He nodded, and handed me back the videocassette Harry

had borrowed. 'By the way, Harry says not to worry about the chip in his CD. It doesn't affect the sound quality.'

'So,' I said, ignoring this and handing him his water, 'what's YPW?'

He chuckled. 'Your Perfect Woman. It's not the best name in the world, but at least it's precise.'

'A dating agency?'

'No, not exactly. But if that's how you want to think of it, that's perfectly acceptable. Shall we start with some questions?'

I sat down in the chair alongside Soumenda. He placed his clipboard down on the black wooden trunk I used as a coffee table. He pointed at the left-hand column.

'This is for your personal details – you can fill it in yourself afterwards. It should be self-explanatory. I've already filled in your address for you, so all you have to do is write in your full name, date of birth, et cetera. But we find that talking through these other questions really helps people formulate their thoughts. After all, this is a big undertaking and we wouldn't want to make a mistake.'

'OK,' I replied, 'so what do you want to know?'

'Let's start at the beginning, shall we? What's your acceptable age range?'

'For a partner?'

He nodded. Many people had suggested I should go to a dating agency. My mother was the most persistent, threatening to sign me up herself if I didn't do it. But after talking to a teacher at my school who used a dating agency, the internet and personal columns to ensure a regular flow of weekend partners, I got the impression that this sort of business was for hardier souls than I. The teacher had tried to make his lifestyle sound like liberated adult fun, and seemed delighted at the prospect of a partner-in-crime, but his persuasive statements ('no one takes it very seriously . . . it's more about finding regular bed-buddies than a future spouse . . .') convinced me that I would feel ill at ease in this world. But as my main reservation was the seediness of searching, I thought that, as the agency representative had come to my house, I could consider going on one date, if the conditions were acceptable.

'How much will this cost?'

'Oh, don't worry,' he replied, 'Harry is handling that side of things. He said to consider this a gift to a kindred spirit. So, age range?'

'No range. I want a woman exactly the same age as me.'

Soumenda nodded. 'Specifics aren't a problem, Mr Ellis. I told you to think of us as a dating agency because that's the easiest way for some people to comprehend what we do, but in reality it's a whole lot more complicated than that. If I've started out by asking you to make broader choices, it's because some people prefer to leave room for . . . a little artistry, shall we say? But if you want to be absolutely exact, well, in a way that makes things easier. So, when you say you want a woman who's exactly the same age as you, do you mean right down to the date of birth?'

'Actually, no,' I replied, enjoying this. 'If things do work out between us, I'm a greedy man and don't want to share my birthday with anyone. Make her one day . . . no, one week . . . older.'

Soumenda liked this. 'OK,' he said, 'once you've filled in your date of birth, we'll work out hers. I'll just make a little note here to remind myself. Now, would you prefer a blonde, brunette or redhead?'

'Redhead, ideally. Or a brunette. Definitely not a blonde.'

He laughed. 'What's wrong with blondes?'

'What kind of blonde are we talking about?'

'Like I said, Mr Ellis, the details are up to you. Ash blonde, honey blonde, peroxide . . . you can specify the exact shade if you wish.'

'The only reason I'm hesistating is that there are some types of blonde hair that I don't mind. Especially that sort of shade which is almost more brown than blonde. I'm trying to think of a good example. What's that actress's name? Michelle Pfeiffer.'

'Is that what you want?'

'No,' I said, shaking my head, 'I don't want a blonde. Blondes are trouble. I'll tell you what I want. I want a brunette who has just a hint of red. A reddy, dark brown brunette. Do you know what I mean?'

'I think so. Eye colour?'

'Blue.'

'Height?'

'Five foot five inches.'

'Breasts?'

I looked at Soumenda. He was sucking his pen and watching me expectantly. Was this the sort of thing they usually asked at dating agencies? I couldn't imagine it was, and tried to make a joke out of it, 'preferably.'

Soumenda smiled. A trail of saliva joined his pen to his lip as he took it out of his mouth. 'I don't need a description, Mr Ellis. But if you'd like to give me a cup size?'

I knew nothing about cup sizes. 'That's OK,' I said. 'I'll leave that detail to you.'

'Come on, Mr Ellis, you've been very precise so far. Why are you getting coy now? You must have a preference? Small, medium or large?'

I sighed. 'Medium, then, but I'm really not that bothered. Actually, no, on seconds thoughts I do have something to say here. I want her to be a real woman, with hips and curves. An hourglass figure. I don't want her to be thin, or boyish, or athletic. I want a woman with a body that has character . . . a body I can love.'

'Whatever you say. Now how would you like her to dress?'

'For our date?'

'No, in general. This is one of the specifications that people usually find difficult. But clothes can make or break a relationship. I understand that you're a modern man and

thinking about these sorts of questions doesn't come natu-
rally, but put all thoughts of sexual equality out of your mind
for a moment and let yourself shift into fantasy mode. This is
your perfect woman, remember, and you can dress her in any
way you wish. Look, if it makes it easier, think of her as an
actress in a play or a film. The choice of clothes helps define
her character. Actually, let's stop calling her "her". What do
you want her name to be?'

'Um, won't she have her own name?'

'Mr Ellis, you decide everything.'

I had already decided that I was only going to endure one
date, so if Soumenda insisted on being silly, then I would be
silly too.

'OK,' I replied, 'Cherry.'

I watched him write C-H-E-R-I.

'No,' I told him, 'not Cheri, Cherry. With two "r"s and a
"y".'

'Is that an American name? Would you like her to be
American?'

'No,' I said, 'English.'

He noted this down in the box for 'nationality'. Then he
said, 'And her surname?'

'No surname. Just Cherry. Like Madonna.'

'Well, your wish is our command, but not having a
surname might make things awkward for the girl. And for
our records, come to that. Are you sure you can't think of
anything?'

'OK. Smith.'

'Smith. Good,' he said, writing this down. 'Now clothes
. . . what's your preference? You can specify a range, or set
certain rules . . .'

'Rules?'

'Yes, for example, if you were very old-fashioned perhaps
you might want to stipulate that Cherry only ever wears
skirts or dresses, never trousers, or stockings instead of
tights.'

'What is this, Soumenda? Russian mail order brides? Call girls? Lonely housewives you've found on the internet? Actresses? A casting company?'

'Oh, I forgot to tell you something. Harry said to tell you that these stipulations are only supposed to be a bit of fine-tuning. We've already studied your scart plug, so to speak, and most of the specifications will be taken from there. So Cherry will already look like your fantasy woman, and only wear what you want her to wear. Any more preferences when it comes to underwear?'

I picked up his clipboard. Sure enough, there was a space left for underwear and four boxes: [ ] expensive lingerie – G-strings acceptable; [ ] expensive lingerie – G-strings not acceptable; [ ] casual; [ ] none. I read this and laughed.

'This is an elaborate practical joke, isn't it? Serves me right for talking to a lonely old man in a bar. Say thanks to Harry, this has been a lot of fun, but I'll have to ask you to leave now.'

Soumenda looked flustered. 'Mr Ellis, please, even if you don't take this seriously, please humour me a little longer. Otherwise there could be terrible consequences for both of us.'

I should have thrown him out then, but I had a sudden realisation that there was something at stake here for Soumenda. Money, probably, for ably acquitting his role in this stunt. Even if I didn't believe a word of it, I was growing to like Soumenda and didn't want him to forfeit his payment.

'OK,' I said, 'I really don't care. You tick one for me.'

He did so. 'I'm glad you're beginning to get into this, Mr Ellis, as we're about to come to the most difficult section of the specifications. To comprehend, that is . . . at least for some people. It's a definition of character and background, I suppose, but it will probably be easier for you if you continue to see it as an accumulation of detail. I'll skip forward a bit so we can start with an easy question. What sort of job would you like Cherry to have?'

'I'd like her to be a teacher so she could get a job at my school. If she's my perfect woman I'm going to want to spend as much time as possible with her, right?'

'Teacher, OK, that's easy. Now what kind of temperament? Do you like submissive women? Or would you prefer someone who could take control of your life?'

'Are there boxes for this answer?'

'No,' he replied, 'you have to give me five adjectives.'

'Oh, OK. Shy . . . honest . . . sincere . . . I suppose this is a contradiction, but I want her to be confident as well . . .'

'We all have contradictions of character, Mr Ellis. One more, please . . .'

'OK, ha ha, rich.'

Soumenda's thin smile betrayed his lack of amusement. 'I'm afraid that's not really a character trait. Don't worry, Cherry will have her own money and you won't be expected to pay for everything, but if you want her to be a teacher she's not going to be rich. Try to take this seriously.'

'OK, I've got one . . . sexual. I don't want her to be a nymphomaniac, but it would be nice if she was interested in that sort of thing. Sexual in the best sense of the word, by which I mean needing sex to be mature . . . although I definitely don't want her telling me about her experiences with other men . . .'

Soumenda raised his hand. 'All I asked for was an adjective.'

We ran through a few more questions and then Soumenda came to his last, and most peculiar, area of enquiry. 'OK, Mr Ellis, we're almost there. All I need to know now is what do you want her parents to be like?'

I looked at him, totally perplexed. But he knew that all he had to do was get me through this and then he could collect his money, so his voice took on a gentle, imploring tone. 'I know how strange this sounds. But all you have to do is think of Cherry as a character again. What kind of parents would your perfect woman have?'

'What kind?'

'Describe them.'

'OK, her father was a circus strongman who died when Cherry was thirteen. Her mother is a trapeze artist, now in her late fifties, a trapeze artist and a tightrope walker. She's quite fragile, and a bit hippie-ish and liberal.'

'Great. That's excellent. Thank you, Mr Ellis. If you could quickly fill in your personal details . . . and may I please use your toilet?'

I used Soumenda's biro to fill out the rest of the form. When he came back out, he took the form, shook my hand and got up to leave.

'So, when do I get to meet Cherry?'

'Soon,' he replied. 'I can't tell you exactly when. But don't worry, Mr Ellis, I promise it'll be a nice surprise.'

I showed him out.

SEVEN

The summer holidays came to an end and I returned to school. In the weeks since Soumenda visited my flat my perfect woman had failed to materialise and I'd come to regard the whole thing as a cryptic practical joke. The punchline – presumably – was that I'd taken Soumenda's questions seriously and was sitting at home waiting for Cherry to show up. There was no doubt that what had happened to me was extremely strange, and I thought it would make a suitable staffroom anecdote, a story to counter everyone else's showing off about their exotic holidays. And at first I believed my story was a hit. After I'd told Tom Carson he kept dragging me across the staffroom to relay the events to the rest of the teachers during the day's subsequent breaks. But soon I realised from their deadpan responses that it was one of those occasions where everyone's acting polite and interested, but you know that secretly they're making fun of you. When the headmaster came over the tannoy to call me to his office, I thought I was going to get told off for fantasising. Especially when Tom said, 'Maybe he wants to hear about Cherry too.'

The worst thing about working as a teacher is that sometimes you feel like you've regressed to being a student again. You know those nightmares you have when you're back at school and you've got an exam you haven't prepared for? I used to have those every night. (I have different nightmares now, of course.) It might have been embarrassing to dream you're in a classroom and you forgot to put any clothes on: it's even worse when you're the naked teacher. And because of the way the system is, and the kind of characters this profession attracts, if you're even slightly rebellious it's easy to feel as anxious about some aspects of school as an adult as you did when you went through the system first time round. Teacher or student, the scariest thing in the world is to be called to the headmaster's office.

The headmaster's name was Fred Lane. He was in his forties, younger than some of the teachers but with an old-fashioned attitude towards education that made him popular with most of the staff and a potential liability for the local education authority. It was no secret that the people in power were keen to close the place down, but before taking this terminal course of action they were parachuting in a last few sacrifices on the off-chance that one of these egotistical superteachers might be able to initiate a miraculous recovery that would stop this school stymieing its success statistics. Fred had never shown any interest in me, which was the way I liked it.

'Steve, don't worry, I won't keep you long,' he said, gesturing for me to sit down. 'Did you have a good holiday?'

I wondered whether he intended this as a cue, but just in case he hadn't heard my story, I simply said, 'Yeah. Not bad.'

'Go anywhere nice?'

I shook my head.

'A holiday at home, then? That can be the best break of all sometimes, can't it? I'd like to do that myself one year, but I can't see it happening for a while. My wife's parents have this place in the South of France and she insists we go there every year. The kids don't like it much, they'd prefer to go to America, and I can't say I blame them, but I'm hoping that giving them an early introduction to Europe will pay off in the long run. I don't know if you agree with me . . . we've never had this sort of conversation before, have we . . . but I think that trying to teach someone French is a fruitless pursuit unless they've at least visited the country. Do you speak French, Steve?'

I shook my head.

'That's OK, it doesn't matter. I'll come straight to the point. As you know, at the end of every winter term we have a school trip to Paris for the students studying French. Obviously we usually send the French teachers, Mme Lalande and M. Lafont, but it's recently come to my attention . . . and I realise this is great gossip, but please don't spread it round the staffroom . . . that Mme Lalande and M. Lafont have been having sex with their students.'

'Students, plural?'

'Two separate students, two separate affairs. I don't know this for a fact . . . yet . . . but the rumours seem to have a certain substance to them.' His voice became meditative. 'All rumours usually do.'

'You mean Mr Jonson genuinely doesn't have a penis?'

He laughed. 'I hadn't heard that one. Anyway, if I had cast iron proof I'd sack both teachers immediately, but there are two other problems that prevent me from taking action. The first is that, believe it or not, French teachers are incredibly hard to come by, especially when the school year has already started, and the other is that these two students are probably our only high-fliers. To be perfectly frank, they really shouldn't be at this school, but both students have lefty parents who believe in the comprehensive system . . . ha ha ha . . . and because they're both quite attractive it doesn't seem to have done either of them too much harm. But, as well as being intelligent and attractive, they're both . . . the boy especially . . . extremely sensitive and I think that if I sacked the teachers and the scandal became public it would cause them both a great deal of trauma and could stop them getting the A grades they're currently cruising towards.

'While I don't want to punish the students, I do want to punish the teachers. I want them to get paranoid and I want them to know I'm on to them. The easiest way for me to do this is to stop them going on the Paris trip. I'm sure they're looking forward to a night in a hotel with their students and this will come as a real shock. The trouble is, the rest of the staff are all potentially just as bad and I don't want to give them the opportunity to create their own scandals. So I've decided to send Tom Carson, as I know he is a completely reliable, happily married man with a wonderful wife, and he suggested you as the best person to go with him. I have to admit I was surprised, not because I don't think you're an honourable and reliable person, but because I would imagine that even the most dutiful husband would have had a crush on one of his colleagues and I expected him to recommend a female member of staff. The fact that he decided on you confirmed his virtue and made me confident this trip will be a success. That's if you want to go.'

He looked at me. I nodded.

'Great. Then that's that sorted. Now, if you'll excuse me, I have a new teacher I need to interview.'

I left his office and walked past the beautiful woman waiting outside. I wanted to get a proper look at her but Fred Lane was holding his door open and standing behind me, so I kept going, not wanting him to think he'd made a mistake in choosing me for the Paris trip.

EIGHT

When I arrived home that evening, the bedroom ceiling fell in. I suppose it was only to be expected, given the house's general state of disrepair. I found my landlord's phone number and gave him a ring.

'Well, Mr Ellis,' he said, after I'd explained what had happened, 'what do you expect me to do?'

'I expect you to send someone round to repair it.'

'Ordinarily, of course, I would be more than happy to do this, Mr Ellis, if, that was, I happened to be dealing with a respectable tenant, but you forfeited your contract with me three months ago when you stopped paying your rent.'

'I didn't stop paying my rent . . . I started withholding it when the hallway ceiling fell down. And I'm going to continue withholding until the ceilings are repaired.'

'Mr Ellis, try to look at this situation from my point of view. What proof do I have that you're going to start paying your rent again? For all I know you don't have the money to pay the rent and you're using the condition of the house as an excuse . . .'

'Of course I have the money. I'm a teacher, I have a regular income.'

'Teachers live in penury, everyone knows that. And who knows, maybe you have a gambling problem.'

'I don't have a gambling problem.'

'Well, even if you don't, are you expecting me to believe that you have the last three months' rent waiting for me in your bank account? I know how this works, Mr Ellis. I send someone round to repair your celing and then you move out and steal my money.'

'If I was going to move out, why would I want the ceiling repaired?'

'You're right! And that would be even worse. I repair your ceiling and then you live there in perfect luxury, rent free.'

'I'd hardly call this luxury. So what are you saying, that you won't repair my ceiling?'

'Not until you pay the rent outstanding.'

I suppose I could have dragged my mattress into the lounge, but I'd had enough of my landlord and the flat, so I phoned my parents.

'You want to move back in tonight?'

'That's OK, isn't it, Dad? I don't have anywhere else to go.'

'Well, yeah, son, of course, whatever you need. But you know that your old bedroom is full of cardboard boxes. It'll take a while to clear it out.'

'That's OK. You make a start and I'll come over and give you a hand.'

I knew my landlord wouldn't think I'd moved out, and probably believed I'd soon back down and pay the rent, so for the moment I stuffed a rucksack with shirts, socks and pants, and took a couple of suits on hangers. Then I picked up the blue CX110 and a handful of CDs and called a taxi.

NINE

It had started to rain heavily. Talkative taxi drivers come in many types: the one tonight didn't believe he was talkative, insisting on how he respected a passenger's right to a silent carriage while he jabbered away as if he'd die of a terrible disease if he didn't tell me his entire life story before I reached my destination. Ordinarily, this would have annoyed me, but leaving my flat had left me feeling oddly liberated and in truth the taxi driver was affable enough, even offering me an umbrella.

'It's OK,' I said. 'I only have to walk up to the front door.'

'It's not a problem, I insist. Besides, it's not mine. A passenger left it in the cab.'

'OK,' I replied, taking it.

I paid the fare and he waved goodbye, driving off into the distance.

My father opened the door and I went inside.

'Mum's out,' he told me.

'Does she know I'm coming to stay?'

'Not yet. But she should be back soon. Have you eaten?'

I shook my head. 'You?'

'No. I was going to order a takeaway, but then you rang and I thought I'd wait for you. Shall we have some food before sorting out the bedroom?'

'Yeah, that'd be nice. What sort of takeaway? Chinese?'

'No, Thai. Direct from a really good restaurant. In fact, it was your friends who told us about it.'

'Friends of mine?'

'Jake and Lauren.'

I had to think for a minute. 'Oh, you mean Tom Carson's friends. I don't know them that well. I've met them a few times at Tom's dinner parties, but that's all. How do you know them?'

'Your Mum does yoga with Lauren.'

'I thought she'd abandoned yoga.'

'That was her old class. That was ten years ago and it was a load of macrobiotic types who kept blowing off every time they put their legs behind their heads. And the final straw for Mum was when her yoga instructor told her he was imagining her naked as she went through her exercises. But her new group's much more upmarket. It was Squirrel who got her back into it again.'

'Oh,' I said, 'I didn't know that. How did Lauren know that Nicky was my Mum?'

'I think it took them a while to put it together. But now they're really good friends. And Jake's a good laugh as well, don't you think?'

'Don't you find them a bit wild? All the orgies and everything?'

'What orgies? They don't go to orgies.'

'Yes they do. Jake told us all about it at one of Tom's parties.'

'Really? Do you think they'd take us?'

'Oh, Dad, don't be disgusting. Do you have a menu for this Thai place?'

The food was as good as Dad had promised. I had Chef's Special Country Chicken and a bottle of Sprite. Afterwards we went up to my old bedroom and started moving the boxes into one of our three lofts. Although I usually tried to spend as little time as possible in the company of my parents I found myself feeling pleased at the prospect of a few weeks in my old bedroom. I didn't have any books to mark and tomorrow was a relatively easy day, so I felt relaxed and even a little smug about the fact that I hadn't caved in and paid my landlord. There was only one thing that worried me.

'Dad, is there a way of forwarding your phone calls? You know, like you can for letters?'

'Yeah. Who are you with again?'

'BT.'

'All you have to do is call up, put a stop on the line and ask for a message telling callers to ring here instead. But are you sure you want to do that? How long are you planning to stay?'

'I'm not moving back into that flat. Whatever happens.'

'OK,' he said, 'then maybe you should leave a message.'

'D'you mind if I go and do that now?'

'I knew you'd find some way of shirking.'

'I'm not shirking,' I protested. 'Besides, don't worry, I'll be right back.'

I went downstairs and made the call. When I came back up, Dad asked, 'So what's all this about then? You're not usually worried about phone calls. Met someone special?'

'No, it's not that. Just . . . well, I took Mum's advice about being proactive.'

'You joined a dating agency?' he laughed.

'Not exactly.'

He looked up from the box he was shifting and asked, 'So what then?'

I knew the minute I started telling him the story that I was making a mistake. It was like being back in the staffroom again, although my father was looking at me with concern rather than amusement. I couldn't understand why everyone thought I was taking this seriously. How did I come across to my friends and family? A naïve idiot? My father had known me all my life, surely he could credit me with some intelligence? Didn't he realise I knew it was all a joke?

'Steve,' he said, 'do you think it's safe giving out this number to these sort of weirdoes?'

'Dad, I know they won't call. But it's like a joke or a game. Just in case it is real, I want to know how it ends.'

'OK, Steve, I won't pretend I understand what all this is about, but please don't tell your Mum, OK? She's already really worried about you.'

I agreed not to say anything, more to appease my father than for any other reason, and we continued emptying the room in silence.

PART THREE

TEN

When I awoke, my mother was trying to pull off my duvet.

'Come on,' she told me, 'don't be bashful. I've seen it all before. Although not for a while, I'll admit. Has it grown in the meantime?'

'Morning, Mum. Can you stop that, please?'

She sighed and sat down on the edge of the bed. Her fine brown hair was clipped up at the back and in need of a wash. 'Poor Stevie, what's going on with you? How come you had to leave your flat?'

'Didn't Dad tell you? My bedroom ceiling fell down.'

'Can't you make them fix it?'

'Yeah, but that's not the point. They're blackmailing me for my rent money . . .'

'And you don't have it?'

'Of course I have it. But I don't want to give it to them. Otherwise, how am I going to make them understand my protest?'

'Aw, honey, what are you protesting about?'

'My landlord doesn't give a shit about his tenants. The hallway ceiling fell down and he didn't do anything; now my bedroom's gone and he's refusing to fix it until I pay him. It's actually a pretty nice house, or would be if he hadn't let it get so run down, and it makes me sick that he cares so little about it . . . and us . . . that he's prepared to let the property run to ruin and endanger the lives of the people who live there.'

Mum stared at me. 'Well, you can hardly expect to get a decent place for the amount of money you're prepared to pay.'

'Yeah, but still . . .'

'So how long are you planning to stay?'

'If I can stay here for a fortnight I'll have a big enough deposit for somewhere decent.'

'Only a fortnight?'

'Yeah . . . I haven't paid my rent for a while.'

'Well, OK, dear, but only if you promise me you're going to start looking for a new place now. You know it can take a while to find somewhere decent and we don't want you moving into another dump.'

'OK, Mum, I promise.'

There had been intermittent storms throughout the night, and every time I'd awoken from another troubling nightmare I'd listened to the rain and used the sound to help me get back to sleep. After eating breakfast with my parents, I picked up the umbrella the taxi driver had given me and headed out to the bus stop.

I entered the staffroom just behind Tom Carson. As I was shaking the rain from my umbrella, he smiled and complimented me on it.

'Very rock and roll,' he said approvingly.

'Rock and roll?'

'Yeah, the black and red and all those little logos. The lips are the Stones, there's Guns N' Roses, look, and Aerosmith . . . but what's that last one, I don't recognise it. RTX? What does that mean?'

'I don't know. It isn't my umbrella.'

'Did you confiscate it from one of your students? Smart move, in weather like this.'

'No. It was a gift from a taxi driver. He told me a

passenger had left it in the back of the cab, but I think it was stolen from a hotel.'

'How d'you know?'

'Look.' I showed him the elegant gold lettering on the black handle of the umbrella: 'The Tenderloin Hotel', followed by a phone number.

'Tenderloin,' said Tom. 'Isn't that a district in San Francisco?'

'Maybe,' I replied, 'I don't know.'

'Let's ask Mary,' he said.

Mary was a geography teacher. She was standing by the sink waiting for the kettle to boil. There was a small patch of dried Tippex in the shape of a map of Africa on the seat of her skirt. Tom and I went over with the umbrella and showed it to her.

'Yeah,' she said, 'it's famous for its prostitutes. But I've read about this hotel in the *Evening Standard*. It's a rock-themed place, the same sort of thing as the Hard Rock Café or Sticky Fingers.'

'Right,' I replied. 'Maybe I should return the umbrella.'

'Are you kidding?' asked Mary. 'They can afford it. Besides, if you don't want it, I'll have it.'

'No,' I told her, 'I want to hang on to it for the minute.'

Mary turned back to the kettle. I was enjoying this unusual moment of intimacy with my fellow teachers and wanted it to continue. I wondered whether Tom fancied Mary and then remembered how the head had been surprised that he'd chosen me to accompany him on the Paris trip.

'Is there enough water for me to have a coffee too?' Tom asked Mary.

'Of course. Would you like one too, Steve?'

'I don't have a mug.'

She reached over the sink and picked up a mug, winking at me. 'Well, we'll just borrow Becky's, shall we? As long as you promise not to tell her.'

Mary made coffee and the three of us walked over to the

large orange chairs in the centre of the staffroom. I sat next to Tom and said, 'By the way, I forgot to thank you for recommending me for the Paris trip.'

'Oh,' he said, 'is that what Fred wanted you for?'

I nodded.

'What did he say?'

I smiled. 'He was really impressed that you suggested me. He said most men would have at least one staff member they wanted to shag . . .'

Mary stopped blowing on her coffee and looked up. 'What's this?'

'Haven't you heard? Jean and Emanuelle have been screwing their students.'

I looked at Tom, shocked. 'I thought we weren't supposed to tell anyone.'

'Oh, Mary doesn't count. I trust her more than I trust my wife.'

'Do you, Tom?' she asked. 'That's nice. So Fred doesn't want them going on the Paris trip?'

'Exactly. Steve and I are going instead.'

Mary looked hurt. 'What about me? I'd do anything for a trip to Paris. Even with the students.'

Tom glanced anxiously between Mary and me. I was pleased to see his smug confidence desert him, and I knew he was worried about how to answer without offending one of us. He tried cockiness, 'Because I knew that's what he expected. And Steve's just confirmed that I played exactly the right card. What did I tell you? I'll be deputy head in no time.'

The buzzer for registration sounded. I thought about what Tom had just said and tried not to feel hurt. We gathered up our stuff and headed off to our respective classrooms, all committing the terrible staffroom sin of carrying our coffee mugs with us.

ELEVEN

'There's someone waiting for you,' my mother told me as she opened the door. I had my own key, but had rung the bell anyway, anxious about walking in on something I wouldn't want to witness.

I assumed it would be either Soumenda or Harry Hollingsworth, either of whom could have tracked me down from my phone message and the new number. But when I went into the lounge I saw my next-door neighbour Len sitting on the sofa in the first small square of the living room, clutching a china mug of tea. I had only seen him on the street before and I felt unsettled at having this man in my parents' house. It was like seeing a wild animal in domestic surroundings, and equally disturbing. My mother stood in the doorway. Len looked up at her and then appealed directly to me.

'All right, lad?'

I nodded, and sat down. 'What's this all about, Len?'

'They're bastards, you know. Landlords. You know Mr Butler is a bloody millionaire. He is. He fucking is. Do you know how many houses he owns?'

Len was always like this. He swore up and down the register without a variation of emphasis, the cuss-words acting more as punctuation than amplification. This meant that you could never tell exactly how angry he really was, especially as the more comfortable he felt the worse his language got. I could see my mother was bemused by this man and possibly a little nervous, even scared.

'Forty-nine, isn't it?'

'Forty-nine. Exactly. Forty fucking nine. That shithead, that fucking cunting wankstain owns forty fucking nine houses and not a single one of them is fit for human habitation. Brian showed me your ceiling . . .'

'Hang on, Len. You went inside my flat?'

'Well, yes, lad . . . I went in with Brian. He had to go in to have a look at your ceiling. Mr Butler told him to do it, after you called him. See, your mistake was to give those tight-fisted crapheads a key. They wanted one to my place too, but I told them to fuck off. Anyway, the point is, I saw your ceiling and Brian said he's been instructed not to do any repairs on your flat until they get the back payments on your rent. Now I know you're not going to pay. That's all right, lad, that's the right thing to do. But you're making a mistake in moving out. You are moving out, aren't you? That's why you've come here?'

'Yes,' I replied, 'I'm not giving them the back payments . . .'

'No, lad, that's right, you shouldn't. But neither should you give up. If you move out now, you've let those tossers get the better of you.'

'So what do you suggest?'

'Ten years ago, Mr Butler was a good landlord. But when he realised that neither of his sons were interested in taking over from him, he gave up. All he's interested in now is selling off his property. It's taking him a while because the deals keep falling through and he's treated his tenants so shittily they're keen to make life as difficult as possible for him, but now he's got some bloody fools who are interested in buying your house, my house and the house next door and turning them into a crappy Montessori or whatever the fuck you call it school. Now, my lawyer has some contacts who have told her that the reason why he's not repairing our houses . . . and our place is just as bad as yours . . . there's windows broken and the central heating is up the spout . . . is that he wants to make as many of us move out as possible and then offer whoever's left a small pay-off. Double the deposit, summat like that. But my lawyer says we're to sit tight. She says the way to get money out of someone is to force it out of them. So this is the plan. You and I call a meeting of all the tenants from your house and my house . . . I think it's about nine altogether, what with all those fucking students downstairs in yours . . . and we agree that what we want from our Mr Butler is nine grand each. Cash, mind, no cheques. Nine grand cash. It doesn't matter to me, none of this don't matter, I've got a house up north I can move into any fucking time I want. But I'm going to make a bloody stand. We're all gonna make a bloody fucking stand. Sit tight and make a stand. And if he don't agree then we'll tell him that two things are going to happen. The first thing is that we're going to make a fucking big story about what a shit landlord he is . . . and I'm not just talking about local press either . . . I'm talking national newspapers and TV.'

'How are we going to do that?'

'Open house, lad. Fucking open house. It's an old northern idea, but up here they won't bloody know what's hit 'em and think it's a fucking genius original concept . . . those fucking students, for one, are gonna bloody love it. What we do, all of us, we turn our homes into like an exhibition space . . . like an anti-Ideal Home exhibition or some fucking conceptual art bollocks. We won't charge anyone to come in. Yes, lad, that's right, no charge. But our houses will be open to the general public. People can go from flat to flat checking out the fucking squalor we live in.'

'And what's the point of this?'

'The point, lad, is that we shame him. This man is dying, right, so he doesn't care about his tenants. But what he does care about is his reputation. He's led a quiet . . . basically, what he sees as a decent life . . . and all he wants to do now is liquidise his assets. People get scared when they're old . . . trust me, lad, I know what I'm talking about . . . especially when their reputations are at stake. So this will fucking mortify him.'

'What's the other thing that'll happen if he doesn't pay?'

'We'll call the health and safety people. If I'm wrong and he doesn't give a shit about his reputation then we'll just have to make things as difficult as possible for him. So what do you say?'

'It sounds like a great idea,' my mother answered for me. 'He'll move back in tomorrow.'

TWELVE

The only problem with moving back into my flat was that it would take them a while to reconnect my phone, especially as there was a red bill I hadn't paid. My mother offered to lend me her mobile, but I told her I'd cope. Two days later, Soumenda reappeared at my door.

'Mr Ellis. Your phone's not working.'

'No.'

'May I come in?'

I gestured for him to follow me upstairs. 'Gosh,' he said when he came into my flat, 'it's dusty in here. Is this all from the hallway?'

'My bedroom ceiling fell down.'

'Oh. May I have a glass of water?'

'Of course. So what's this about?'

'You're not a very curious man, are you, Mr Ellis?'

'What d'you mean?' I shouted from the kitchen as I filled a glass with water.

'Cherry. Your perfect woman. Haven't you wondered why you haven't met her yet?'

'Oh,' I replied, returning, 'I just assumed it was a joke.'

Soumenda accepted the glass. 'A joke,' he repeated, eyebrows rising. 'Why did you think it was a joke?'

'Well, she didn't show up. If it was real I thought I would have met her by now.'

'You would have done. If you'd paid more attention.'

'I don't understand.'

'We gave you the clue, Mr Ellis. It's up to you to solve the mystery.'

'I'm a busy man. I don't have time for solving mysteries.'

'Be that as it may, this is getting expensive. You have another week, Mr Ellis. If you haven't worked it out by then, I'm afraid you'll never meet Cherry and that'll be the end of it. I'm sorry.'

'It's OK. You shouldn't feel guilty. You played your part exemplarily and if you want me to write a note to Mr Hollingsworth confirming that fact I'd be happy to do it. But you chose the wrong man. You're right. I am incurious. I detest crosswords and riddles . . . I've never had the patience for chess . . .'

He raised a hand. 'It's really very simple, Mr Ellis. I'm sure you'll work it out.'

I didn't reply. Soumenda finished his glass of water, placed it back on the black wooden trunk and stood up. I showed him out.

After he'd gone, I realised what he was talking about. Soumenda was right: it was obvious. Not that I would ever have worked it out on my own, but only because I didn't know I was in the middle of a mystery. But if I looked at my life as if it were a computer game, I had only accumulated one special object recently. The user hint was in Soumenda's words: we *gave* you the clue. It was in the corner of my room, standing against the wall. I went over and checked the black handle again. 'The Tenderloin Hotel', and a number. I took the umbrella with me and went out into the street, looking for a phone box.

I didn't find one until I reached the end of my street. And then something strange happened. I picked up the receiver as normal and listened for a dialling tone before inserting my coins. Instead of a tone I heard someone say, 'Bob, what the fuck is that noise?'

'Sounds like traffic.'

'Do you have a window open?'

'No, I fucking don't. It's you, isn't it, you're doing something?'

Both voices sounded so angry that although I couldn't help feeling curious I had to replace the receiver. The concept of a crossed line seemed ridiculously archaic and I decided instead that someone must be tapping this line deliberately. But why were they doing this from a phone box? And why had the listener abandoned his post? Was that how the police did things these days? I knew the men on the other ends of the line didn't know who I was, but I still felt scared. I hated being implicated in situations that were nothing to do with me. I pushed open the door of the phone box and went across the road to the next booth.

I dialled the number on the umbrella's handle. The man who answered said, 'Hello, Tenderloin Hotel.'

'Hi. I was just phoning because . . . well, I found one of your umbrellas. Actually, that's not true. I didn't find it. A taxi driver gave it to me.'

He laughed. 'I see.'

'Anyway, the point is, I'd like to return it.'

'That's really not necessary, sir. We're a rock and roll hotel. If you want to throw your television out of the window you won't hear a word of complaint from us, and the umbrellas are complimentary.'

'I'm sorry, I don't think you understand. The taxi driver who gave me that umbrella, I think he was in the employ of a man named Harry Hollingsworth.'

'Sir, I have no idea who that is.'

'OK. Maybe you're not in the loop. Can you call your manager . . . or anyone who is in a position of power . . . and ask them if they've heard of him?'

He hesitated, then said, 'That name again, sir?'

Slowly and deliberately, I enunciated, 'Mr Harry Hollingsworth.'

'I'm going to have to put you on hold, sir.'

There is a certain pressure in being chosen to take part in this sort of game. As a child, my favourite programme was 'The Prisoner', which I caught on one of its many repeats. As much as I enjoyed this television show, I never warmed to Number 6. Patrick McGoohan was a glowering, scary actor and his monomania terrified me. The Village seemed a perfectly pleasant place to live, filled with attractive women who spoke with cut-glass accents and seemed likely to be sexually obliging in interesting ways. But now I was having my own experience of being manipulated by forces outside my control, I understood his truculence and felt close to sharing it, no matter how desirable an enticement my controllers had prepared for me.

'Hello?' said the voice on the other end.

'Yes.'

'I'm the front desk manager of the Tenderloin Hotel. And I can tell you with some certainty that no one here has heard of a man named Harry Hollingsworth.'

'It's OK, you don't have to talk to me as if I'm insane. I'm phoning because I have an umbrella of yours and I want to return it.'

'You don't have to.'

'I want to.'

There was a long silence on the other end of the line.

'OK.'

'So can you give me directions?'

'Of course, sir. Where will you be coming from?'

PART FOUR

THIRTEEN

The Tenderloin Hotel was in the centre of town. Ordinarily I would have taken a bus, but tonight a taxi seemed more appropriate. I was half-expecting the same driver as last time, but maybe they thought that was too obvious. Or perhaps they were worried that he couldn't be trusted to resume his role and might give something away under my interrogation. This driver barely spoke, and I didn't bother engaging him in conversation. But he did know where the hotel was before I gave him directions, confirming my suspicions.

The taxi stopped outside the hotel. I paid the driver, then went through to reception. A wicker basket alongside the glass double-doors was stuffed with umbrellas, but I carried mine across to the reception desk. The man there said, 'Good evening, sir. Would you mind waiting there a minute? The front desk manager asked me to contact him when you arrived.'

'If he's the front desk manager, shouldn't he be here?'

'He usually is, sir. But tonight there was a problem in one of the rooms. If you'll just wait there.'

He picked up the phone and dialled a short number. He covered his mouth as he spoke so I couldn't see what he was saying. I felt insulted, but didn't complain. He replaced the phone, turned to me and said, 'If you'd like to go through to the bar and order yourself a complimentary drink, he'll be down in a minute. Just tell the waitress it's on Zak's tab.'

'His name is Zak?'

'No. It's just a name we use. Like a code.'

'Oh.'

'Order whatever you like. Don't choose something cheap just to be polite.' He gave me a knowing smile. 'If I may make a recommendation, the apple martini is exquisite.'

I walked away. I didn't want an apple martini. There was a pink neon sign above the entrance to the bar that read: 'The Tenderloin Joint'. I wondered whether the reference to meat was deliberate. Probably not. It seemed a fairly humourless place. What kind of clientele came to a hotel like this? Presumably not teachers, but I doubted whether rock stars did either, unless they were desperate for attention. No, I guessed most visitors to the Tenderloin Hotel were business-men trying to be ironic or trendy, or fashion victims. No doubt they tried to market it to the Americans or Japanese, but I couldn't see that working. The bar probably did better business than the hotel. It was certainly busy tonight. Only one empty table. I sat at it and flipped through the drinks menu, before deciding to stick with beer.

'Are you sure that's all you want?' the waitress asked.

'Positive,' I replied. 'By the way, this is on Zak's tab.'

The waitress narrowed her gaze. 'Are you a friend of Zak's?'

'Zak doesn't exist.'

'He doesn't?'

'That's what they told me.'

She nodded and returned to the bar as I tried to work out what the music was. I'd heard it before, but not for a long time. People had played it at university. One of those records you heard coming out of people's rooms or at parties, but never bothered to buy.

A man approached my table. He was overweight and wearing the hotel's supposedly stylish black and purple uniform so I assumed he must be the front desk manager. He offered me his hand. 'I'm Simon. Thanks for returning the umbrella.'

'That's OK.'

'You really didn't have to, you know.'

'I know. I wanted to.'

He stared at me. 'It really is very unusual, you know. Someone being quite so conscientious.'

'It seemed important.'

The waitress came across with my beer. For some reason, although it was all she was carrying, she still had it perched on a black plastic tray.

She smiled at Simon. 'Do you want a drink, Si?'

He shook his head. The waitress placed my beer on the table and walked away. Simon sat opposite me, tugging at his trouser legs as he lowered himself onto the stool. I picked up my beer bottle and took a swig from it.

'What's your name, sir?' Simon asked me.

'My name?' I asked. 'Don't you already know it?'

'I don't think so. Did you give it at reception? I'm sorry, sir, they didn't pass it on.'

'It's Steve.'

'And what do you do, Steve?'

'I'm a teacher.'

'Are you? That's a good job. I wish I did something like that.'

'Don't you like your job?'

He sighed. 'There is an art to it. But it's hard to do the things I'm good at, the things I'm trained to do, in a place like this. A rock and roll hotel is a perfectly acceptable concept, but most of the guests use it as an excuse to act like pigs.'

'What are the things you've been trained to do?'

'Stage management. That's the art of being a front desk manager. What it boils down to. Keeping everybody moving, soothing tempers, making sure everybody's in the right place at the right time . . .'

'And is that what you're doing with me?'

Before he could answer, another uniformed man appeared behind him.

'Si,' this man said, 'we've got a problem in Room 407.'

'OK.' He turned back to me. 'Please don't feel you have to hurry, Steve. Relax, finish your beer, and if you feel like another, it's on Zak.'

He smiled and walked away.

FOURTEEN

They timed it beautifully. Just as I was about to finish the last swallow of my beer, she sat down opposite me. I hadn't noticed her approach, but now she was at my table I could barely breathe. I'm not someone who finds many women attractive. In fact, part of the reason I've stayed single so long (aside from social ineptitude) is that I have a very narrow concept of beauty and can't be bothered to seduce someone unless they fit my exact criteria. (In this, Harry Hollingsworth had chosen the perfect person for his plan.) And even then, the illusion is usually destroyed when I start arguing with the woman. I put my empty beer bottle down and stared at her, unable to speak.

'Can I sit here?' she asked.

I nodded. It wasn't just my specifications that made this woman beautiful, but their subtle innovations too. I'd asked for a brunette with a hint of red, but I had said nothing about hair length. Cherry had gorgeous shoulder-length brunette hair, loosely curled: a stray tendril highlighting the pale beauty of her neck.

'You know who I am, don't you?'

'Cherry?' I croaked.

She laughed. 'That's right.'

'I didn't think . . . it's taken so long . . . I wasn't sure . . . Why here?'

'It's just one possible beginning, Steve. It has to start somewhere.'

I nodded. 'So what happens now?'

'That's up to you.'

'Are you staying at the hotel?'

'I have a room here.'

'Can we go up to it?'

She raised one full, but perfectly groomed eyebrow. 'You don't want to talk?'

'I want to talk all night. But not in front of these people.'

'OK, Steve. Whatever you want.'

I got up from the table and followed Cherry out of the bar and across the reception floor to the lift. Walking behind her, I thought about all the other specifications Soumenda had persuaded me to set. They had made a big fuss about my video of clandestinely filmed women being my scart plug but, today at least, Cherry wasn't dressed in a particularly eighties style. Or, at least, not in a way that looked noticeably anachronistic. In fact, she was dressed incredibly simply, wearing a blue denim jacket over a white top with an opal crucifix attached to a slim silver chain around her neck. Her black skirt ended just above her ankles. She turned and looked at me.

'I'm on the sixth floor.'

'OK.'

The lift doors opened and we had that moment of embarrassment that you always have when you're suddenly in a small space with someone you find sexually attractive. Only it was even more intense than usual because of the strangeness of the situation. I wanted to give in to the fantasy, but before I could do that, I had to be certain that Cherry felt something for me. The truth behind this set-up no longer worried me: I didn't care whether she was a prostitute, an actress, or simply someone Harry Hollingsworth had bribed to have sex with a stranger. But I needed to believe that she felt something towards me: that she wasn't simply playing her part in the way Soumenda had. It had been a long time since I'd last been with a woman – nearly twelve years – and the sense of physical urgency I felt in that lift could easily have unmanned me, but before I could do anything with Cherry, I had to try to find out something about the real woman beneath this manufactured illusion.

We reached the sixth floor and the lift doors opened. Cherry went out first, pointing down the corridor. 'It's number 622.'

I followed Cherry to her room. She was walking quickly and seemed excited. She took a keycard from the pocket of her denim jacket and slid it into the slot. Then she pushed the door open and went inside. I noticed two large empty suitcases by the mirrored wardrobe.

'How long have you been here?'

She smiled. 'Well, it did take you a while to find me.'

'Are you getting paid by the day?'

Cherry turned round. 'Don't worry, I have enough money to see me through. And I start teaching on Monday.'

'Teaching?'

'Yes. At your school, like you wanted. You know, you walked past me when you came out of Fred's office. I was dying to say something then, but I thought it would spoil it.'

'Spoil what?'

'Our first date. Or meeting, if that's what you'd prefer to call it. Would you like a drink, Steve? It is Friday night, after all.'

Cherry sat down on the king-size bed. She lifted up her left foot so she could unbuckle her black leather shoe. I sat in a black and purple chair by the window. Cherry reached down, unbuckled her other shoe, then gave both sets of stockinged toes a firm squeeze. She looked at me, waiting for an answer to her question about the drink.

'Do you have any CDs?' I asked.

'Not of my own. But the hotel provide them. Along with

this . . .' She lifted a small brown paper bag with something obscene jutting out between the handles.

'What's that?'

'The S&M bag. Free with compliments from the Tenderloin Hotel.'

'Like the umbrellas . . .'

'Exactly. We thought it was more tasteful than giving you a dildo.'

'Do the dildos have telephone numbers on them?'

'I don't know. Let's have a look.' She emptied the paper bag onto the bed. There were two dildos, a tube of lubricant, a blindfold and a pair of handcuffs. Cherry examined the dildo. 'Yes,' she said triumphantly, 'what great advertising.'

'Cherry,' I began, holding her gaze, 'I am enjoying this, but you've already given the game away by saying "we" just now, so you might as well tell me what this is all about . . .'

Cherry pushed herself down the bed so she could sit with her back against the headboard. 'There's nothing to give away. When I said "we", I was referring to me and Harry Hollingsworth. And you already know I know him.'

'Know him?' I replied. 'So you're a friend of his?'

'Not exactly. He's my father . . .'

'You're his daughter?'

'In a sense. But, then, in a way you are my father too. You gave the specifications, he created me.'

'So that's the fantasy, is it? You're a robot?'

'Isn't that what you wanted? My name . . .'

'What about your name?'

'I thought you gave me this name because you were making a reference.'

'To what?'

She shook her head. 'It doesn't matter. I made a mistake. No, Steve, don't worry, I'm not a robot.'

'So how did he create you?'

'Let's not talk about that. I can tell you about my real parents, if you want.'

78

'Oh, yeah, right. The circus strongman and the trapeze artist . . .'

She looked hurt. 'This is supposed to be enjoyable, Steve. For both of us.'

'Is it enjoyable for you, Cherry? Do you find me attractive?'

'Of course I do. Any woman would . . .'

'Then why have I been single for the last twelve years?'

'Don't be angry with me . . .'

'I'm sorry, Cherry, but . . .'

'Steve, can I tell you something about myself? Something that I think will make you feel a lot more comfortable?'

'Is there beer?'

'Pardon?'

'In the mini bar? I'd like a beer.'

Cherry stared at me for a moment. Blue eyes, just as I had specified. But there are different shades of blue, and if her eyes had been a scary cadet blue I would have immediately felt alienated from her. No, Cherry's eyes were just a shade away from midnight blue, so that each pupil was not that much lighter than its iris. In spite of everything, her eyes engendered trust.

She broke my gaze and moved across the bed so she could lean down and open the plywood door that hid the mini-bar. She looked through the refrigerated chamber and brought out a glass bottle of Michelob. 'Is this OK?'

'It's fine.'

She opened the bottle and handed it to me. I took a long gulp and asked her, 'So what did you want to tell me?'

'A personal trait of mine.'

'OK.'

'I never lie, Steve. I'm incapable of it.'

'Then tell me the truth,' I snapped.

'I am, Steve. But you must take what I'm saying seriously. When I say I never lie, I mean ever. White lies, lies of omission, I can't do any of them. It's caused me a lot of trouble in the past, but I can't help it.'

'So your name really is Cherry?' I said in a sarcastic tone. She didn't reply.

'This is ridiculous.'

'Steve, think of it as a dream. Or, better still, a game. Since the moment you met Harry, you have been presented with a series of possibilities. This is just your latest choice.'

I put down my beer. 'Then I choose to leave.'

FIFTEEN

The moment I left the hotel room, I felt afraid. I was convinced someone would try to stop me, and that they might use force. When I reached the ground floor I avoided the lobby and went through alongside the bar, looking for a rear exit. I found one next to a small internet exchange and used it. Now I had returned the umbrella, it was raining heavily. I walked past the blue plastic dustbins to the main road, where I was relieved to see several taxis with their lights on. I hailed one, and climbed in the back. The driver turned and asked, 'Where to, mate?'

I told him. He scowled. I found his irritation reassuring; at least I could be sure he wasn't in on the scam. I thought about Cherry's last words and the difficulty of arranging a game like this – if that's what it was. I could see how it would be possible, if you had the time, money and inclination, but surely there were too many variables to exercise anything beyond a minimal element of control. Sure, you could set up the board and read out the rules, but how could you persuade someone to play?

The taxi driver didn't talk. When we reached my road, I paid him and went up to my front door, unlocked it, and walked up the stairs to my flat. There seemed more dust in the air than ever. I could hear music coming from the students' flat downstairs. I unlocked both locks on my door and went inside. The flat felt cold. I went through to the small side room and turned the heating on.

I felt a certain pride that evening, sitting watching sitcoms I never normally would have bothered with. Most men would have gone ahead and slept with Cherry, or whatever she was really called. But I was a disciplined man, albeit a very lazy one. This was how I stayed single for twelve years. I wanted Cherry, she was the sexiest woman I'd ever seen. But no one was going to manipulate me.

I was strong.

Disciplined.

Disciplined and strong.

SIXTEEN

Of course, if our situations had been reversed and I was Harry Hollingsworth, I probably wouldn't have worried. God can't watch us all the time. There's no such thing as free will: just the duration between our desires arising and our decision to fulfil them. Time. That's all that separates us from the mice.

I'm not a patient person. If something doesn't happen immediately, I assume it's never going to happen. Obviously, this is stupid. But I live entirely in the present. Which makes my current situation difficult. Although writing this is proving more therapeutic than I ever could have imagined. You should have told me that. For the first time, I can see my life as a narrative. It was Harry Hollingsworth who introduced structure into my life.

So, while I was disciplined and strong on Friday, by eleven pm Sunday I'd lost all my previous resolve. The only question that remained was whether Cherry would still be in the hotel room. To be on the safe side, I used a different cab company and when the driver arrived he needed directions. When we reached the hotel, I swept through reception and went straight up to Room 622, still uncertain about whether I'd find my perfect woman or a perfect stranger.

Cherry answered the door on the second knock. She was fully dressed and embraced me without saying anything. We went inside. I had decided I wasn't going to argue with her any more, and had only one question.

'Can I do what I want with you?'

She looked nervous. 'What do you want to do with me?'

'Do you have a hairbrush?'

She nodded. 'In the bathroom.'

I walked through to the brightly lit bathroom and took Cherry's hairbrush from the white counter by the sink. The handle was thick, rounded and smooth, with a gentle curve at the end and soft flexible ridges. There was a fuzz of hair caught between the beaded spikes. I pulled off as much as I could and dropped it in the toilet bowl.

Cherry was sitting in a chair, waiting for me. I went to the window and drew the curtains, which were still open, in spite of the late hour.

'What do you want to do with me?' she repeated.

'I want to get you ready for bed.'

Cherry looked up. I knew she was surprised, but I hoped she wasn't frightened. I was impressed at her willingness to put herself in such a vulnerable position. I supposed it was no different from every other time a woman was alone with a man she didn't know in a hotel room, and maybe Harry Hollingsworth had already given her background information on me. I walked round behind her. She was wearing a silk spaghetti-string pale blue top. I started to brush her hair. At first I began another stroke whenever I hit a tangle, but then she said, 'It's OK, pull it hard. Get the knots out.'

I brushed harder, creating small crackles of static. It was so long since I'd been close to a woman that this was almost more exciting than a cuddle or a kiss. Not that I didn't want that form of intimacy too. I stopped brushing and kissed the crown of her head. Then I gripped the sides of her top and slowly pulled it up over her body. I placed my hands lightly on her warm, smooth shoulders, gently kissing the small grooves there. She shivered, and I started to slowly kiss her neck, my fingers stroking her sides and the soft curve of her belly.

I came round from behind her and knelt on the carpet.

Cherry turned her bum towards me so I could undo the button and lower the zip of her black skirt.

'I'm so glad you came back,' she told me.

'Me too,' I said, one hand stroking the inside of her thigh as I slowly tugged her skirt down. She stepped out of it and I ran the brush's spikes over the backs of her thighs. I remembered Soumenda's stupid list of specifications and my reluctance to engage with them, and then realised which box he must have ticked: Cherry was wearing black string knickers with an elegant silk trim. I kissed her pale white buttocks, lifting the brush up higher and turning it so I could rub the rounded back against the soft mound of her knickers. She seemed to like this so I continued doing it, at the same time moving up to lay gentle kisses along the line of her spine.

'Do you have pyjamas?' I asked. 'Or a nightdress?'

She shook her head. 'No. I hate wearing anything in bed. Even knickers.'

'Then I guess these should come off,' I told her, putting my thumb inside the thin elastic.

She turned and looked at me. 'You can do anything you want.'

'It's about you as much as me,' I told her firmly. 'It has to be. If it's not, it doesn't mean anything. That's my fantasy.'

Cherry nodded. 'I understand. This is a good beginning.'

'You have to tell me things. It's twelve years since I've been with a woman.'

If this surprised her, she didn't comment on it, saying only, 'What you're doing with the brush is nice.'

I felt like I'd exposed myself, so I retaliated by tugging down her knickers. I pulled her legs slightly apart then reached behind her back and unclasped her bra. I dropped onto the floor and ran the brush's beaded spikes over her belly and then up to her breasts. I gently brushed the spikes across each of her nipples.

She stopped me for a moment, gripping my face between her hands and kissing me properly. The kiss felt more shocking than anything else we'd done. Being single for over a decade changes a person: you feel like you've forfeited the right to any physical contact for the rest of your life. Even if a woman smiles at you when your bodies accidentally brush together in a crowded tube, you still feel like you've committed a hideous crime. Because in that instant you're terrified the woman has sensed the corrosive power of your lust.

Earlier I wrote that the last time I dated women was at university, but the way I expressed myself made it sound like this was the only time I dated women, and that's not true. I actually lost my virginity at an extremely young age. Thirteen. This is how it happened: my parents were worried that I wasn't making friends at school, so my mother bribed one of her friends to persuade her son to play with me. As much as my mother enjoyed teasing and manipulating me, I don't think she had any sense of what her friend's home was like. The friend was someone she'd known since she was ten, who'd given birth to her son the same year my mother had given birth to me, and by this time their friendship was limited to the odd phone call about parents' evenings or choice of sports kit. But this woman's son made an effort with me, and not just because my mother had given me sweets and crisps to share with him in playground breaks. Before long, we became genuine friends and he started to stay over at my house. One night, he asked me to come to his home instead, and I was astounded by what I witnessed. The carpets had been torn up from the floors, leaving dusty patches of black underlay throughout the house. My friend had a makeshift go-kart made out of scrap wood and perambulator wheels with a rusty nail in lieu of a seat that he dragged in circles around the lounge. His father lay asleep on one sofa, an empty brown glass bottle of Dry Blackthorn by his chair. His mother slept on the other, mummified in a stained blue sleeping-bag. My friend phoned his cousin,

Shelly, and she came over with another girl. Leaving his parents to sleep undisturbed, the four of us bedded down on a dirty double mattress in the spare room. We started the evening by playing a game where one of the boys had to touch his girl somewhere on her body and the other girl had to guess where he'd touched. I was touching Shelly; my friend the other girl. But we were both too timid for the girls' appetite, touching shoulders, toes and knees, and they made us swap over so that the girls were now touching the boys, and all Shelly kept doing was grabbing my cock and balls, laughing every time her friend guessed correctly. Before long, the game had been abandoned, and Shelly was initiating me. I was hopeless, already overstimulated by the touching game and embarrassed by my friend's experienced movements on the bed beside us, and when I came in a couple of quick minutes, I felt more relieved than upset. But the unsatisfied cousin stretched out my cock and forced me to fuck her again. This time I managed five minutes. She laughed when I came and, after smoking a cigarette, got back on top of me and fucked me again, this time going so slow that it was two hours before my final, pitiful ejaculation.

I didn't visit my friend's home again. For some, this evening might sound like a fantasy situation, but the whole experience had left me traumatised, and when I finally got another girlfriend, at fiteen, she was astonished that all I wanted to do was kiss. We kissed for hours at a time, through whole films or boring lessons. We snogged until our stomachs growled, a strange situation I've never experienced as an adult. The same thing happened with my next girlfriend, and the next, until one day I started to hate being kissed. It suddenly seemed incredibly intrusive: a horrible violation. Since then, I had never really enjoyed kissing as much as any other sexual activity. Which was another reason why my subsequent assignations were so short, as there's much less kissing in the average one-night stand. But when Cherry kissed me it brought back the sweetness of those original teenage kisses and I felt a scary return of my adolescent submission opening up inside me.

I still had the brush. I gripped it tightly, even as Cherry embraced me. She was on all fours, with me lying beneath her. I let her hold me, then moved the brush to my crotch, pointing it upwards. I wasn't sure what I was doing. The kiss had changed the temperature of the moment, altering our interaction from erotic fantasy to sexual intimacy. I had once received through the mail a brown paper pamphlet advertising a man's health workshop entitled 'Beyond the Pornographic Impulse'. I don't know who sent it to me, but I'd always assumed it had been one of my female students. Now I wondered whether it had been Harry Hollingsworth: if this set-up had actually started long before I met him. It was true that in my years without a woman my fantasies had frequently been shaped by material created out of empty anger and pain, and it was in an attempt to legitimise (in the sense of seeking a female response to) this form of frustrated lust* that I acted now, bringing my hips up so the tip of the brush handle pressed against Cherry's labia. She reached for the small tube of lubricant that had fallen from the S&M bag, uncapped it with one hand and rubbed a couple of squeezes over her clitoris and inside her vagina, then, while I remained in the same position, reached down and guided the soft flexible ridges inside her, until, at a certain shallow depth, she stopped and touched my chest, warning me to leave it exactly where it was. Cherry slowly inched her naked bum up over my clothed chest (and there was something wonderful about this juxtaposition) and we rearranged ourselves so I could lick and kiss her thighs. Soon, I moved up to the area around her vulva, blowing lightly on the skin

---

* I worry this will be misunderstood. I didn't want to hurt Cherry, but I had this idea, this possibility – oh, why is it so difficult to express moments of extreme sexual intimacy without seeming trivial – and while I was ready for my movements to be rejected, I had to see what would happen.

there while she gently jiggled the brush handle. I rubbed some extra lubricant on my fingers and slowly stroked her clitoris with the lightest of feather touches, feeling it gently extend. I pulled her body towards me and began to kiss and lick her clit, concentrating my entire being on managing the right lightness and soft attention. It had been so long since I had done this and I realised that, although it was only a physical reaction, if I could make Cherry come it would serve the same purpose for my ego as any psychological revelation. Cherry squeezed out the brush handle and gripped my fingers, bringing them up so I could touch her inside instead.

As I slid two fingers inside her, Cherry said, 'I thought you were supposed to be getting me ready for bed.'

I looked up at her. 'You mean you don't have someone doing this for you every night?'

'Oh,' she said, 'please don't stop. I'm sorry for distracting you.'

'Mmm,' I said, continuing with what I'd been doing. Cherry arched herself upwards, her thin, elegant fingers moving up to stroke her breasts while I sucked her. The opal ring on her middle finger emphasised her nakedness. The inside of her vagina began to tighten around my knuckles. Her clitoris felt full between my lips, and I realised she was getting close. But in the next few minutes, something seemed to go wrong, and I noticed the previous mounting tension dissipate. I wondered whether I should ask what I'd done wrong, but although her breathing had slowed, Cherry was still fingering her nipples so I decided to continue. I tried to make my tonguing more direct, but slightly lighter, hoping for a signal that would prove I was still doing the right thing.

I kept licking and kissing until a few minutes later, when Cherry used her hands to stop me. I rolled away from her, upset by my incompetence. She noticed my disappointment and asked, 'Steve . . . what's wrong?'

'I'm sorry, it's been so long. I wish I was better.'

'What d'you mean, better?'

'I wanted to make you come.'

She laughed. 'Steve, I came three times. Two little ones and then a medium-sized one. I only stopped you because my legs were turning to jelly and I couldn't take it any more. It's been a long time since I last had sex too.'

'Really?'

She nodded. 'Almost four years. I had a lot of energy stored up.'

'And that's the truth? Not part of your persona?'

'I told you, Steve, I never lie.'

I sighed. Cherry lay supine beside me and reached for my hand. I stared at the ceiling and said, 'That's one thing Soumenda didn't ask me to specify. Smell.'

She laughed. 'You could have done, if you wanted. I have a friend who designs perfumes. He could probably produce almost any scent you wanted.'

I turned on my side, placing a hand on Cherry's belly. This was one of the first real clues she'd given me, certainly her furthest deviation from her set script. The fact that she knew someone who designed perfumes, and that this person could have been employed in the deployment of this scam seemed incredibly revealing.

'And will I get to meet this friend?'

'If you want. But it's entirely up to you. I know how annoying it can be when you've just met someone and they suddenly expect you to get on with all their mates. I'm happy with it being just you and me for now.'

'I see.'

Cherry's fingers progressed to my fly. 'Enough talk. You must be desperate.'

'For what?'

'Your turn.'

'No.'

'No?'

'Not tonight. I don't want you to do anything to me tonight. In fact, I don't even want to take my clothes off.'

Cherry seemed to pick up on the edge in my voice, but to her credit, didn't attempt to move. Her naked body really was perfect, a full figure with proper curves and weight where there should be weight. I ran a hand over her flesh and then hugged her close to me. She accepted the embrace with a sigh of relief.

'It's OK,' I told her. 'This must seem weird to you, but it isn't really. I just need some time to adjust to this. How long do I have you for?'

She laughed. 'You have me forever. Till death us do part.'

'How much does that cost? How much are you getting? How much is a life worth?'

'Please don't talk like that, Steve. Not after what we just did.'

I nodded, accepting this. My fight wasn't with her. And I wasn't going to send her away. If I had any chance of solving this mystery, it was best to keep Cherry close. Not just for the secrets she might reveal, but because if I played along, Harry Hollingsworth would think he had won.

And as soon as he thought he was safe, I would strike.

SEVENTEEN

Sometimes I imagine the Hollywood version of my story. They wouldn't be able to do the sexually explicit bits, not in such detail, not if it was going to be a mainstream film, which I think it should be. But without the explicit sex, this story would work in a much more straightforward way. As prose, I'm worried my case will collapse, unable to support the weight of these eccentric sex scenes, but unfortunately they are essential to my case.

Thinking about how what happened between me and Cherry and Harry Hollingsworth could be adapted for film reveals the huge division at the heart of all cinema, stories, and, indeed, life. It's an artificial division in life, but of huge significance in art. I'm talking about the schism between the Hollywood romance and hardcore pornography, or literary erotica and the love story or, even, the public and private. These are debates that have taken place elsewhere, and while I have nothing that could be said to be truly new to add, I have to reformulate some past theories for myself before we can move on.

The reason why neither the conventional love story nor the hardcore pornographic movie completely satisfies is because the division of the natural pairing of love and sex has made each separate part seem strange. The brutality of pornography stems from the fact that these films are dealing only with the mechanics of sex, and without depicting love the only virtue they can emphasise is willingness, and it is hard to look at these performers and feel anything beyond a sympathetic affection for them. The emptiness of a love story comes from our inability to imagine the actors in bed together, even when we know this is exactly what is happening in real life, off-screen. It's actually hard, and almost always horrifying, to imagine people we know in bed together. And although some women like to boast of the intimacy of their conversations with their female friends, even this divulgence counts for little as they are not privy to the private thoughts of their partners. What woman truly knows what her lover is thinking while he is inside her, or she is using her fingers to bring him to orgasm?

You could reverse the gender in this question and present it to me, in relation to Cherry, but I would counter that this is the exact matter of this account. In these first few encounters, Cherry remained a complete enigma to me. And yet our relationship progressed solely through sex, and the next scene began when I awoke to find that Cherry had unzipped my trousers, slid my cock through the slit in my boxer shorts and was now holding it and staring at me.

My eyes hurt. I blinked, and she took this as a sign of assent. Her first few strokes were soft, gently ungluing my helmet from its foreskin. She was still naked and I suddenly felt very silly to be wearing my clothes. I raised my hips and she pulled my trousers down.

She had to guide the material of my underwear back around my hard cock, but once she'd done that, she threw my boxer shorts and trousers onto the floor. Stripping my socks from my feet, Cherry dropped the black balls alongside the bed and started to wank me with a firmer grip. The only problem was that she was putting the emphasis of each stroke in slightly the wrong place. It didn't feel painful, just slightly odd, and if she carried on like this it would take me forever to come. Still, her inexactitude made me feel happy because it had happened with women before and the reason why was that, as if in compensation for the rest of my physical shortcomings, I am larger than most men. I'm not saying I'm freakishly huge, but my penis looks more like the after pictures in the penis enlargement adverts. Not in a grotesque or frightening way, but enough to give a potential partner pause. I'd assumed that Cherry would be so experienced that she'd know exactly where to touch me, and the fact that she didn't increased my affection for her.

I put my hand around her fingers. This worried her, and she looked up at me, asking, 'Don't you want me to?'

'Yes,' I told her, 'it's just, you're not quite doing it right. The sensation is a bit dull there.'

'Oh,' she said, 'OK, show me . . .'

I guided her hand and she continued with a steady speed, watching me the whole time. I felt the beginning of a mild cramp in my leg, but this increased the pleasure rather than distracting me. Cherry swapped hands, using the other to uncap the lubricant. Liberally squeezing it over her finger, she reached beneath me and slid this digit into my anus. I felt a pleasing pinch, and Cherry smiled and dug in deeper, aiming straight for the inner bulge of my prostate gland. This dazed me and I stared at Cherry's breasts, noticing how large her nipples were and how dark they seemed against the whiteness of her ample flesh. It wasn't that I was judging her body, just getting used to it. A form of submission. Accepting the role written for me. Her finger was now pushing inside me with real purpose, and she was stroking my cock with increasing speed. Suddenly I was at that wonderful moment when the orgasm has started but there's no physical evidence. Cherry used this frozen moment to kiss me. Then, when the sperm flew across my chest, Cherry's soft hot tongue immediately lapped it up.

'You don't have to,' I told her.

'No,' she said, 'I know. But I want to know what you taste like. Next time I'll give you a blowjob . . . I know they're nicer . . . but I wanted to see what your eyes looked like when you knew you were going to come.'

'What time is it?' I asked.

'Eight o'clock. Have a shower and I'll call a taxi to drive us to school.'

EIGHTEEN

In the taxi we talked about what attitude we should adopt to each other in school. Cherry suggested it might be best to pretend we didn't know each other and feign a slow courtship over the next few weeks. But I was so pleased to finally have a girlfriend, even under these strange circumstances, that I refused to indulge in any subterfuge. 'I want to rub their fucking noses in it,' I told her, 'especially Tom Carson.'

Cherry looked concerned. 'But won't they think it's odd? I start teaching at this school and you're already going out with me?'

'They already know all about you.'

She looked shocked. 'What? How?'

'I told everyone in the staffroom about Soumenda's visit. It was a running joke for a while. But I have a good way round it so people won't think it's completely weird and we only have to bend the truth a tiny bit. Remember when you came in for your interview, and we nearly met? Well, let's just say we did meet then, but the whole thing was staged. My story was a joke, about Soumenda, I mean, a silly stunt the two of us thought up together when we first met.'

'When?'

'In the summer holidays. Where's your house?'

'What?'

'You must have lived somewhere before you moved into that hotel.'

96

'My lease was up. I have all my belongings with me in the Tenderloin.'

'Those two suitcases? That's all your stuff?'

Cherry nodded. 'More or less.'

'What about your parents?'

'My Mum lives in Chessington. I'd have to get up at six in the morning every day if I was going to get into school from there.'

I shook my head. 'No, no, I don't mean that. We've already decided you're going to move in with me.'

Cherry looked surprised. 'Have we?'

'Yes, that's what you said just now, isn't it?'

'Well, all I meant is that's what people would assume if we came into school together on my first day. I didn't know you were going to let me . . .'

'Let you?' I laughed. 'Wait till you see my flat. But what I was asking was, do you have a room at your parents' house? A base? Somewhere you started from?'

'Are you investigating me again, Steve? I'm happy for you to meet my mum.'

'What about your dad?'

'He's dead.'

'Right. The strongman. I forgot.'

The taxi dropped us outside the school gates. The kids lurking there straightened up when they saw Cherry and there were several wolf-whistles. As we passed closer to the students, I heard a tall, thin boy I didn't know hiss, 'Slut.'

My hand shot out in an instinctive gesture, grabbing him around the windpipe. I pushed his back against the white metal bars, choking him and screaming in his face, 'Take that back, you fucking prick. Tell her she's pretty.'

I was gripping the student's neck so tightly that he was struggling to breathe, let alone speak. One of his friends grabbed my arm, saying, 'Leave him alone. He was only mucking about.'

I didn't like the colour the student's face was turning, so I let him go. He dropped to the ground, fighting for breath. Then he stood up and got close to me. 'I'm going to have you for that. My father . . .'

'Fuck your father. Tell her she's pretty or I'll break your nose.'

Cherry grabbed my arm. 'Steve, it's OK. He's just a kid.'

The student sprinted away from me, turning to shout, 'You're fucking mental. I'll make sure you lose your job.'

'Yeah, whatever,' I said, walking away.

Cherry ran up behind me, saying, 'Thanks for sticking up for me. But hasn't that kid got a point? Won't you get in trouble for strangling a student?'

'That kid won't report me. And if he does, I've got you as a witness. It never happened.'

'Steve, I told you, I can't lie. I'm . . .'

'Incapable of it. Right. I forgot. Well, don't worry, I'm sure it won't come to anything. That kid won't want it known that he called you a slut. They don't look kindly on that sort of talk in a school like this.'

The adrenalin was still surging through me when I entered the staffroom. It was ten to nine and most of the teachers had already gone off to their classrooms. But the person I wanted to run into was sitting with Mary, the geography teacher, on the green and red imitation leather chairs in the centre of the staffroom. Tom Carson was wearing a black suit that was obviously two hundred pounds more expensive than mine (and I'd put on my best to visit Cherry on Saturday night). I stared at his curly brown hair, waiting for him to look up. When he did, I moved in.

'Tom, Mary, this is Cherry Smith.'

'Cherry?' asked Tom, smiling.

'Yes. She's starting here today.'

'Really?' Tom asked, extending a hand. 'What subject?'

'Religious studies.'

'We don't teach RS at this school.'

'It's only going to be a small A-Level class. Five students. Fred said he was coming under pressure to provide the class because the students have influential parents.'

'No students at this school have influential parents,' he said crossly. 'Is this all you're doing? It seems rather a waste of resources.'

'No, no,' she said, 'I'll be teaching a general humanities class as well.'

'But I'm head of humanities,' protested Tom. 'Fred hasn't said anything about this to me.'

'Oh,' said Cherry. 'I'm sorry, I didn't know. We should get together for a talk.'

Tom still looked perplexed. 'I don't understand. Who are you replacing?'

'No one. Fred said he's been worrying about the streaming of the Year 9 and 10 students for some time. He thinks the classes are too big and the differences of abilities too wide. So he's turning the three classes into four. I'm going to take the second to top class.'

'Do the students know about this?'

'Not yet. There's going to be a special assembly this afternoon.'

Tom scowled. 'Fred could have told me first. I'm going to have to change all my lesson plans.'

'I'm sorry,' said Cherry. 'Maybe I shouldn't have said anything.'

He shook his head. 'No, I'm very grateful you did. I just can't believe Fred didn't think it was worth warning me about this.'

Cherry tried to smooth things over. 'I think it was a spur-of-the-moment thing.'

'Nevertheless,' he replied, 'this is the sort of thing I should know about.'

'So which humanities group will I be teaching?' Mary chipped in.

'Who knows,' said Tom. 'This is such a mess.'

Just as Tom's moaning was really beginning to bore me, the buzzer sounded. Cherry glanced at me with a look of relief, and we went off to our various classrooms.

NINETEEN

Cherry and I walked home. My stomach felt tense, anticipating another verbal attack from one of the male students loitering by the school gates. (All day they're desperate to go; tell them they can leave and they want to hang around.) But no one said anything. Maybe news of this morning's incident had spread.

'How was your first day, Cherry?' I asked her.

'Not bad,' she said. 'I didn't enjoy the humanities lesson, but the RS group were good fun.'

'Where did you teach before?'

Cherry looked at me as if I was trying to catch her out. 'Steve, I didn't teach anywhere before. You know my qualifications are faked.'

I sighed. 'I've been having a hard job getting my head around exactly how this scam works. Did Harry Hollingsworth pay Fred Lane to employ you?'

'Fred and Harry are old friends.'

'Really?' I asked, astonished.

'Harry knows everyone in this area. His grandson goes to our school.'

'So Harry is a millionaire?'

'Maybe. But he's not ludicrously rich. He's just a normal businessman. There's nothing sinister about the way he operates. You know how London works. People with similar interests gravitate towards each other.'

'Did you know Fred before your interview?'

She shook her head.

'What about the job? Is it a totally invented position?'

'More or less. I studied theology at uni, so I do at least know what I'm talking about. Fred called one of the students, a popular boy, into his office, and put the idea of doing RS into his head. He told his mates, four of them wanted to do it, hey presto, we have a class that needs a teacher.'

We reached my road. I brushed Cherry's hair to one side and whispered into her ear, 'Take off your knickers.'

'What?'

'Just take them off and give them to me.'

'Here in the street?'

'It's OK. Do it subtly. There's no one around.'

Cherry stared at me. I marvelled once again at the beauty of her face: her high, smooth forehead; thin arched eyebrows; blue eyes; medium-sized noise, straight and perfectly rounded at the tip; and full, large, delicately lipsticked lips. For the first time, she seemed to be appraising me. I suppose it was the request that did it. Maybe she was worrying that I was a sex maniac. But before I had chance to doubt myself, she smiled and reached up under her skirt. Her knuckles moved beneath the black material and seconds later her hand emerged, dragging her knickers down her legs and over each of her shoes as she stepped out of them. Then she handed the knickers to me. They were blue lace: expensive, old-fashioned.

'What's next?' she asked.

'Let's go inside.'

It was partly a diversionary tactic, putting off the moment when I would have to explain about the state of my flat. I gave Cherry the keys and told her to unlock my door. As soon as she'd gone inside, I walked up behind her, pushing her against one of the hallway walls. I hitched up her skirt, and there it was: her beautiful, full, pale bum. I dropped to my knees and buried my face into her, freezing when I heard a cough from the living room.

'Who the fuck's there?' I shouted in a – literally – muffled voice.

Len appeared in the hallway, seconds after I dropped away from Cherry and let her skirt fall back down. 'All right, lad? Brian let me in. I tried phoning fucking hundreds of times, but no one answered, and I had to speak to you before the others arrived.'

'What others?'

'S'all right, lad, they're not coming until six, but I also had to get the food laid out. Mrs Wesley's made fairy cakes and little cocktail sausages. I like little cocktail sausages best, don't you? I don't mean best compared to other sausages, like a big fat Walls' or whathaveyou, but compared to other party snacks. Fucking lovely.'

'Len', I said sternly, 'you can't just keep coming into my flat when I'm not here.'

'Yeah, well, it's Brian who you should be angry at for that, lad, not me.'

'But Brian's not in my flat.'

'Yes I am,' shouted Brian from the bedroom. 'It's terrible, this ceiling, isn't it?'

'Len, who's coming at six?'

'The other tenants. It's nine altogether, unless those students have got any other bleeders hidden away. I told you all this before. It won't take long. All we have to do is get everyone together and agree that what we want is nine grand each. Cash, mind, no cheques.'

'Len, why aren't we having the meeting in your flat?'

'Oh, no, we couldn't do that. No, no, no, I'm sorry, for one thing it's nowhere near big enough. Besides, you want all the others to see the state of your ceiling. You'll see inside my flat soon enough, lad, if we end up having to move to stage two.'

'Open house.'

'That's right, lad, open house. But you're forgetting your manners. Who is this beautiful young lady?'

Len and Brian stayed in my flat for an hour before the other tenants arrived. The students were the first to come up. Only three of them, *pace* Len's silly talk. Two dark-haired girls and a blond boy. Next came Mrs Wesley, who'd prepared another tray of sausages. The Spanish man from upstairs brought two bottles of wine with him, which was helpful as I didn't have anything for my guests to drink and all Len and Brian had between them was four cans of John Smith's. My neighbour from the other side of the hallway brought a CD and I had to explain to him that this was a meeting, not a party. The last man to arrive was a scary-looking punk who lived in the basement of Len's house. I guess he'd already included us two when he said there'd be nine of us.

There were no representatives from the house next door to Len's. When I asked him about this, he said, 'Those bloody fools have already moved out. It's them what started all this.'

'Did they get any money?' the punk asked.

Len shook his head. 'No, of course not. You can't expect to get any money unless you're prepared to make a stand.'

The meeting dragged on until nine, by which time I was exhausted. All we had to agree on was that we were going to tell Mr Butler that we wanted nine grand each before we would leave, but somehow this prompted an argument that lasted for nearly three hours.

When we'd finally turfed everyone out, Cherry turned to me and said, 'I know that was really tedious, but the whole time I kept thinking that as soon as everyone had gone you were going to fuck me for the first time. The tension was unbearable, Steve. I don't think I've ever felt so turned on. Every time you touched my hand I felt I was going to burst into flames.'

I groaned. 'I'm sorry, Cherry, I feel exhausted. I'd love to fuck you, but I don't want our first time to be connected to that terrible man.'

'Oh,' she said, clearly disappointed, 'you don't want to do *anything*?'

'I'm sorry, I'm so tired.'

'How about if we watch each other masturbate?'

'Well,' I admitted, 'I'm not too tired for that.'

Cherry laughed, and ran into the bedroom, pulling me behind her.

That night I had a dream about Cherry. At first I thought it was actually happening, but the dream soon grew so violent that I knew it couldn't be reality. Len returned, rushing into our bedroom with a baseball bat. Dragging Cherry from the bed, he made her stand in the middle of the room while he repeatedly struck her head. After several hard hits, the plastic outer casing of her head split in two and fell away to reveal an old-fashioned black camera, whirring away as it focused on me. The most disturbing part of the dream was that even when the camera had been revealed, I still felt exactly the same about my lover.

PART FIVE

TWENTY

Judith met us at the door, holding her arms out and proffering her cheek for a kiss. It was the first time she'd encountered Cherry, although I was certain Tom would have told his wife all about my new girlfriend. After Tom's initial anger at the rearrangement of the humanities classes, he and Cherry had now become close friends. He was still surprised that I'd made up such a strange story about how we met, but I think it just confirmed his impression that I was a bit eccentric. I was amazed, and proud, that their friendship hadn't provoked jealousy. This was mainly because Tom's friendship with me had changed in quality since he'd met Cherry. Before, it had been obvious that he felt sorry for me. Now he saw me as an equal, and enjoyed the fact that the three of us were envied by the rest of the staffroom, most of whom hated each other.

'Judith, I'd like you to meet my girlfriend, Cherry.'

Judith smiled. 'I feel as if I already know everything there is to know about you, although I know that can't be true. My husband may be a garrulous man, but there's lots of things he doesn't notice. He couldn't tell me one thing about what your voice was like.'

'My voice?' asked Cherry.

'Judith's a speech therapist,' I explained. 'For her, a person's voice is the most important thing about them.'

'Well, that's not entirely true either. Cherry's so beautiful it wouldn't matter if she spoke like David Beckham.'

'Are we the first to arrive?' I asked Judith.

'No, no, Jake and Lauren are already here. Shall we go through? Tom's just popped out for another bottle of wine. I told him we had more than enough but,' she leaned in close to Cherry and said in a conspiratorial voice, 'I think he wants to get you drunk.'

Cherry lowered her head and took my arm. We went through to the lounge. Jake and Lauren stood up. Lauren kissed me and I introduced them both to Cherry.

'I had no idea you knew my parents,' I told them.

Jake played with the zip on his shirt. 'We saw them last night actually.'

Lauren hit Jake with the side of her hand. 'Jake ... I'm sure Steve doesn't want to hear about that.'

'Hear about what?' Judith asked.

'It wasn't full on,' Jake laughed. 'The playroom was really tame. And all your parents wanted to do was watch.'

'What's this?' our hostess prompted again.

'Oh God,' I said, 'my Dad said he was going to ask you to take him. I really don't want to know.'

Lauren put her hand on my arm. 'Steve, I promise you, he's making it sound much worse than it was. It's just a club we sometimes go to. Just like a normal nightclub, but with a few ... extras. But all any of us did was watch. And not even *watch* in that sense. It's more like a cabaret club than anything else. We took your Mum's friend, Squirrel, as well. We went after yoga. I know it sounds odd, but actually it's a really nice way to wind down.'

Jake smiled. 'Although I have to admit I was rather surprised at how much your Dad liked William.'

'Please,' I said, 'you're not telling me my Dad's bisexual now?'

'And what's wrong with being bisexual?' demanded Lauren testily.

'Nothing. But this is my Dad ...'

'Relax,' said Jake, 'he's not bisexual . . . as far as I'm aware. William is a man who punches people.'

'This sounds extraordinary,' Judith laughed. 'The life you all lead.'

'Jake met William at Cambridge,' Lauren explained. 'They both used to perform "services" for a girls' sex society. That's where Jake picked up all his bad habits. What was it called again, honey?'

'The Thélèmites. It's from Rabelais, I believe. Is that right, Steve? You're the English teacher.'

'I've no idea. I've never read anything written any earlier than the nineteenth century.'

'Is that true?' Judith asked. 'Even at university?'

'Oh, I didn't read anything at university.'

There was a clatter as Tom returned through the front door. Judith shouted at him in an excited voice, 'Hurry up, Tom, you're missing all the sex talk.'

Tom arrived carrying two bottles of wine that had been wrapped in brown paper. 'That started early. What's this all about?'

'Jake and Lauren took Steve's Dad to a sex club last night. Apparently he was rather enamoured of a man called William who . . . punches people, did you say?'

'Let's sit at the table,' Tom suggested. 'This sounds like a conversation that should be continued over food. Hi, Cherry, by the way.'

'Hi, Tom,' she replied, letting him kiss her cheek, and handing him the two bottles of wine we had brought.

We sat down. Jake waited while Judith went out into the kitchen and brought the starters through. He leaned back in his chair, aware that he had the attention of everyone around the table. 'William . . . is a lovely guy who used to work as an actuary, but now has a job at this club where he punches people in the stomach. It's very strange. He wears a black hood and trousers and has a bare chest like an old-fashioned executioner . . . like you'd see in a "Hagar the Horrible" comic strip, or the other one, what's it called, with the King? "Wizard of Id", is it? And what William does is, for twenty minutes every night he stands on stage and anyone in the audience who wants to can come up and get punched in the stomach. Only once, but he does it so hard that sometimes people vomit, or fall over.'

'This is a sexual thing?' asked Judith.

'Not exactly. It's more like he's providing a service.'

'A "Fight Club" sort of thing?' Tom suggested, using his trendy teacher voice.

'No, you're not allowed to hit back. It's a punishment. It can be self-inflicted, or a test. Sometimes a woman will get her husband to go up. Or a husband his wife.'

'A test of strength?'

'Um, I'm not explaining this very well. Lauren . . .'

She put down her spoon and looked at Tom. 'The problem with the way S&M is portrayed in the media is that you only ever see these images of skinny men licking a dominatrix's stilettos, or schoolgirls getting spanked. But there's a whole other side to this world that rarely gets explored. Most of the people we've met through clubs or the internet are very intellectual, highly emotional individuals. And almost all of them have suffered from having very liberal, passive-aggressive parents who wouldn't have dreamed of smacking their children, but nevertheless tortured them emotionally almost every day. Punishment should serve the same purpose for an atheist as confession does for a Catholic.'

'Go on,' said Cherry. 'I can use this in my RS classes.'

Lauren gave Cherry a chilly smile. 'If you're punished for something, that's the end of it. The guilt has been transferred. But parents who don't smack their children don't want to relinquish their power. They're control freaks.'

'Did your parents smack you?' Cherry asked Lauren.

'No,' she said, 'but that isn't why I do the things I do. What William is doing, in a way, is absorbing people's sin. Of course, not everyone wants to be punished. Some people just want to prepare themselves in case they end up in a real fight. They're conquering their fear of pain.'

'Anyway,' said Jake, 'it wasn't that your Dad got off on seeing people being punched. But after the session, William came over to our table, and he and your father talked about stocks and shares. The funniest moment was the look of surprise on your Dad's face when he saw William's face after he took off the mask. Because without the mask, William looks like the straightest guy you've ever met.'

Judith laughed. 'Isn't that always the way?'

I was quiet for the rest of the meal and hardly said a word to Cherry in the taxi home. When we were alone in the lounge (where I'd been sleeping since my bedroom ceiling fell in) Cherry touched my hand and asked, 'What's wrong?'

'Doesn't it disgust you? My parents going to clubs with people they barely know to watch a man in a mask punching strangers in the stomach?'

'Does it disgust you?'

'It makes me sick.'

'Why are Tom and Judith friends with those people?'

'I don't know. Makes them feel young, I suppose.'

Cherry kissed me. 'I love you, Steve.'

'When I was eight years old there was this building site near our house. The builders didn't work at weekends and there was this small rectangular space made out of metal and breeze blocks that I liked to crawl into and read books. One Saturday I took some books and Coca-Cola and sandwiches and crawled into this space and as I did so I ripped my trousers . . . they were green cords, I remember . . . and I was so sad that I ran home, and on the way I passed this girl from the neighbourhood. She was sexy and she liked to make fun of me, and I found her really threatening, but I was bawling my eyes out, like someone had died, and she kept asking me what was wrong and I wouldn't tell her. I'd torn away the whole seat of my trousers and I was terrified of her seeing . . .

so I carried on running and then I went into my house and my parents were there and I told them what had happened and I was terrified my Dad was going to be angry, but he said it was OK, he'd buy me a new pair, and I was so relieved that as I walked out into the hallway I started laughing, just out of relief, and my Dad came running after me and because I was laughing he really was angry and I was so scared I couldn't speak or explain and he hit me and said that his father would have been really angry if he'd ripped his trousers and would have made him wear them anyway, and if I thought it was so funny maybe I should be forced to wear ripped trousers too and he hit me again and my Mum came out and I thought she'd come to stop him but the pair of them just started laughing and then she grabbed the trousers and kept ripping and ripping until they completely tore away and I was standing there in my pants.'

Cherry stared at me. I thought she didn't understand. Neither did I, really, and I had no idea where that repressed memory had come from. But then she said, 'I hate your parents. Let's never see them again.'

At that moment, I knew I'd found the true love of my life.

TWENTY-ONE

It had been three months since Mr Butler had refused our request for nine grand each. At Len's urging, we had started our 'open house' campaign immediately. He'd done a fantastic job of publicising this 'happening', taking to PR with an enthusiasm he'd only previously displayed for cussing like a pirate. We had visits from journalists from *Time Out*, the *Evening Standard* and all the local papers, plus two camera crews and a woman from Radio 4. But in spite of all this publicity, so far we hadn't had one visitor to examine the state of my bedroom ceiling. The first TV crew had pulled in some people from the street to pretend to be looking around, but aside from that no one had taken advantage of the viewing times Len had stated on the yellow posters pasted to every lamppost. And that was just the way we liked it.

Len had had plenty of visitors to his flat, but that was because he spent his days on the street outside stopping strangers and forcing them in. Cherry and I just listened out for the buzzer and, very occasionally, left the door on the latch.

When I was twelve, I read our *Family Health* book every night. I was especially interested, obviously, in the chapter concerning sex. The only thing I remembered from the book was a statement about premature ejaculation. In a tone more appropriate to an urbane *Playboy* article than a medical textbook, the doctor wrote that 'while premature ejaculation may be an embarrassment to some younger men, the truly expert lover should be able to train himself to put off his own orgasm until his partner is satisfied'. After that first time with my friend's cousin, I never had any trouble putting off orgasms, but only on rare occasions did I climax through intercourse alone. And I'd assumed that after so long without sex, years of masturbation would have made it even harder. But the amazing thing about fucking Cherry was that I came every time. Sometimes before her, usually afterwards, but always close enough for neither of us to feel overtaxed. It was amazing the benefits being sexually compatible gave a relationship. It felt like a celestial blessing, and completely destroyed any doubts I had about going along with this scam. The first time I ejaculated into Cherry, I had a feeling of cosmic oneness I hadn't experienced since I first discovered masturbation. Cherry felt me orgasm inside her and this triggered her own response and then that was it: everything illicit or strange or fucked up about our coupling had disappeared as we suddenly took on new roles in this drama. No doubt this wasn't as novel an experience as I imagined. I bet the same lightning struck on the honeymoon night of certain arranged marriages, providing a happiness more solid than any liberated love.

That morning we made love as we usually did before breakfast on Saturdays, and Cherry then got out of bed and went from the lounge to the bathroom. She returned almost immediately, lifting her foot onto my bed.

'Do you think this is anything?'

'It's your foot,' I said, silly from sex.

'No, look, my little toe.'

'Which foot?'

'Right.'

I examined her right foot. The nail of her little toe was jet black and almost entirely divorced from the nailbed with a thick wodge of red blood beneath it. All that kept it attached was a tiny sliver of skin.

'Christ,' I said, 'that looks painful. Did you bash it?'

'Not that I remember. But maybe I didn't notice. You know what I'm like at night.'

This was true. Cherry got out of bed three or four times a night to urinate, and every time she banged around in the darkness without paying any attention to what she was doing. It was perfectly plausible that she'd hit her toes without noticing and only just discovered the consequences.

'What should I do?' she asked.

'I don't know. Do toenails grow back if they drop off?'

Cherry shook her head. 'I don't know.'

'Well, perhaps you should put a plaster on it. Keep it attached for as long as possible.'

'Yes, OK,' she said, and went to the small drawer in the bathroom where I kept my meagre medical supplies. Then she came back and handed the box to me. 'Can you put it on?'

'OK,' I said, and did so, kissing the toe as soon as it was covered. Cherry smiled and got back into bed, and we made love again before eating a breakfast of bagels and bacon. Then we went out for a walk.

TWENTY-TWO

Two weeks later, all of Cherry's toenails were black. When she pulled off the plasters the nails came with them, leaving ten furry craters, which made Cherry cry for an hour. It wasn't so much the pain, but the loss. I understood how she felt, remembering how miserable I'd been as a child when I got my first filling. I told her she had to see a doctor and one morning she went to the surgery three streets from my flat. When she came back, she had cheered up.

'It's OK,' she said, 'the doctor said they'd grow back.'

'Did he say what might have caused it?'

'He said I must have banged them without noticing. Or that it might be something to do with my shoes. Or maybe someone stamped on my feet.'

'But that doesn't explain why the toenails went black one at a time. Did you tell him about your other ailments?'

'Please, Steve, don't depress me. It's nothing, OK? I'm perfectly healthy.'

But Cherry didn't seem healthy. She was as sickly as Ren from 'Ren and Stimpy', always under the weather with one problem or another. We had a running joke where I would say to her, 'Oh, you *are* sick,' in a silly voice like Henry does to the baby in 'Eraserhead'. But these pop culture references didn't make it any easier to cope with the fact that there seemed something desperately wrong with Cherry. In the short time we'd been together, she'd suffered from blasts of

IBS, cystitis, diarrhoea, bleeding haemorrhoids, severe migraines and temporary hemianopsia. She also suffered terribly with a bad back, but I think that was down to our sleeping arrangements. Most of her conditions she tried to hide from me, but occasionally she'd get scared and want to talk about it. I think she felt guilty that her corporeality got in the way of her being the fantasy object she was supposed to be. Our relationship had developed, but she still seemed to feel she had something to prove. I assumed that it was because she was being paid to be my perfect woman, but as I kept telling her, once you've found your erotic ideal, all you ask is that she doesn't betray you.

The thing that worried me most was Cherry's hair loss. It was probably the least dramatic of all her symptoms and hardly seemed to concern Cherry at all. She hated her hair, saying it was like 'dog hair' and got everywhere. The latter was true. I first noticed this when after every blowjob I found thick brown strands wrapped around my helmet. She thought this was disgusting, but I enjoyed the cutting sensation as I pulled the hair away. It also clogged all the drains, covered my clothes and came off in small clumps on her pillow. The loss wasn't that noticeable on her head, but I was convinced that this was further evidence of serious sickness.

I was still in bed when she got back from the doctor, and pulled back the duvet so she could get in with me. She moved with incredible caution, gingerly sliding her feet under the covers.

'Cherry . . . are you sure you can't tell me the truth? I don't want there to be anything between us.'

'Steve, there is nothing between us. You come in my cunt, I share this bed with you every night, I haven't held back on any aspect of my personality.'

'What about those specifications I made?'

'Oh, I abandoned those ages ago. I'm not psychotic, Steve, I can't make up a false version of myself.'

'But I don't understand. What is Your Perfect Woman? Is it a real agency? There's no phone number for it, it's not on the internet . . .'

'Look, Steve, forget the mystery. I used to work for Harry Hollingsworth, I had a normal executive job. And then he asked me to do this.'

'But why?'

'Because I fitted your specifications. If you'd asked for a blonde or a redhead, you would have got a different woman.'

I shook my head. 'This isn't a criticism, Cherry, but I can't understand why on earth you would do it.'

'Oh, come on, Steve, you're not that different from me. I had a boring life before, and Harry gave me the opportunity to change everything. It was an adventure. And if it hadn't worked out, I could have stopped it that first night.'

'But how long is it going to continue?'

'Forever, Steve. Harry Hollingsworth has stopped paying me, the mission is over. Everything I do now I do out of my own free will.'

That afternoon, Len came round and told us he'd decided to abandon the 'open house' regime. It didn't seem to be having any influence on Mr Butler, who had proved to be much less concerned about his image than Len had previously believed. It was time for the final stage of his attack: threatening to call the Health and Safety people.

'But I need you to come round to my flat and do it with me,' he said. 'He won't pay any attention if it's just me on my own.'

'We can call here, Len. I don't mind you using my phone.'

Len looked both ways, then scuttled over to the table and picked up the receiver. 'Come on, lad, stand near me. Let's see what this fucker's got to say for himself.'

He dialled Mr Butler's number, saying to me, 'This is a special line. He hardly ever picks up on his normal number, the fucking shifty cunt . . . oh, yes, is that Mr Butler? This is

Len. What? Yeah . . . Brian gave it to me. OK, I was just phoning to say that my solicitor has recommended that, following your failure to respond to our requests, I should call the Health and Safety people. What? OK, the requisite authorities. No, don't you fucking worry, I've got their number. Yes. OK . . . but you should know that it's not just me making the complaint. Yes, that's right, Mr Ellis is with me now.' He stopped talking for a moment, staring at me as he listened to Mr Butler. 'I see . . . yes, OK . . .' He handed me the phone. 'He wants to talk to you.'

'Hello, Mr Butler . . .'

'Mr Ellis, you are aware that as it's now over six months since you stopped paying your rent, I would have been well within my rights to have evicted you a long time ago?'

'Yes, but . . .'

'You are also aware that the man you have invited into your house is a dangerous lunatic?'

'He's your tenant, Mr Butler.'

Len looked up. 'Is he talking about me? What's he saying, the slimy cunt? Don't you listen to a word he says, lad. That man is a compulsive liar.'

'Be that as it may, Mr Ellis,' he continued, 'I am nevertheless prepared to come to an arrangement with you. If you wish to stay in the flat, I am prepared to repair the ceiling and forget about the arrears . . . call it a payment to you in recompense for dust damage . . . provided, that is, you start paying your rent again as normal from next month.'

'When will you repair my ceiling?'

'Brian can start today, if you want.'

'OK.'

'You're not making an arrangement with him, are you?' shouted Len. 'Don't make a fucking arrangement.'

'Oh, and one more thing, Mr Ellis. Mr Hollingsworth asked me to pass on his warmest regards.'

Hearing this name again made me shiver, but I managed to say, 'Thank you, Mr Butler,' before putting the phone down.

Len was furious. He called me a traitor and wouldn't stop swearing. I apologised for a while, then got fed up and asked him to leave. As soon as I got him out of the house, I told Cherry, 'Harry must have intervened. They're repairing the ceiling and Mr Butler's wiping off all the unpaid back rent.'

'That's great,' she said, 'let's go for a drink to celebrate.'

TWENTY-THREE

Brian repaired the ceiling in time for Christmas. Since we'd decided we hated my parents, we were spending the break alone. Cherry rarely mentioned her mother, and I worried that she didn't want me to meet her because it would destroy the carefully constructed illusion. But, equally, I was so pleased to be sharing Christmas with Cherry alone that I didn't bring it up.

Cherry and I spent more time in each other's company than most couples. Aside from when we were teaching classes, the two of us were always together. We had few friends, and they were all people Cherry had met through me. Yet our relationship didn't seem claustrophobic. Cherry was never happier than when the two of us were alone together, and if I didn't try to get her out of the house occasionally we might have spent every day indoors. When I was single I never wanted to go out, but that was due to the embarrassment I felt about being alone. Now I had Cherry, I revelled in the coupley things I never wanted to do before. We went out for meals twice a week, visited the cinema every time there was something either of us wanted to watch and even went for the occasional long walk. We were the perfect couple.

Although Cherry seemed to be happy spending Christmas alone with me, she was slightly more nervous than usual. She'd become emotional in a way that struck me as entirely out of character. Admittedly, Cherry was increasingly frail due to her physical ailments, but I thought she understood me. I am a lazy man, and when it's up to me I always avoid anything that demands practical skill. My flat is full of evidence of my lethargy, from the trails of toothpaste down the inside of the sink to the imprint of my body on the sofa. Cherry had never complained about any of this, and seemed to have a similar attitude towards housework as me (i.e. if I needed a plate, I'd wash one). We usually ate takeaways, from a wide variety of nearby establishments, and both of us hung up our suits or smart clothes and left everything else trailed across the floor. I think Cherry may have initially been surprised at the extent of my selfishness, but she'd adjusted to it over time and now we got along fine when it came to domestic duties. Some people might have been horrified by the way we lived (I dunno, we never had anyone round), but I think our lifestyle is more common than these people realise, especially among those of my sort of background.

Anyway, whereas Cherry was usually happy to slob along with me, she was extremely disappointed that I wasn't at all excited about (or even interested in) the trappings of a traditional Christmas. Every time she mentioned getting a tree, or decorating the flat, I kept quiet, hoping she didn't mean it. We got three Christmas cards between us (one from Tom and Judith, one from my parents and the other from Harry Hollingsworth) and I thought it best to keep our celebrations to a minimum. I enjoyed eating the odd Christmas lunch sandwich from Pret A Manger, but apart from that assumed I could ignore the whole thing.

Nevertheless, I am not a cruel man, and when I realised just how much this seemed to mean to Cherry I went with her to buy a small tree (thirty pounds!), decorations and fairy lights. The next thing that Cherry got excited about was making Christmas lunch. And here she did go overboard. Not only did she want to buy a turkey, a glazed ham, mince pies and those sausage 'n' bacon combos that Cherry called devils on horseback and I called pigs in blankets, but she also insisted on going to specialist shops to buy ingredients for two recipies she'd found in the *Delia Smith Complete Cookery Course* she'd bought especially from a second-hand bookshop just for this purpose. Although I grew testy after a long day's shopping on the twenty-third of December, by Christmas Eve I was pleased by the effort she'd made and looking forward to three days of isolation from the rest of the world.

The Christmas lunch Cherry cooked was incredible. I may have moaned about the extent of her preparation, but it definitely paid off. I'm not a big fan of food, but occasionally even I have to acknowledge that it can serve as something more than mere fuel. I think my fear of gastronomic indulgence is my mother's fault, but in this particular instance I'm not sure why. I ate everything Cherry put in front of me and then sat down with her to watch television. All of Cherry's previous anxiety seemed to have disappeared and I was ready to declare this my best Christmas ever when the doorbell rang.

My first thought was that this was Harry Hollingsworth, or his envoy, Soumenda. Cherry seemed thrown into panic, and said to me in a scared voice, 'Don't answer it, don't answer it.'

I went to the window. My parents were on the doorstep. They were dressed up like carol singers, with my father wearing some sort of comedy top hat and carrying a cardboard lantern. They didn't notice me at the window. I turned to Cherry and said, 'It's my Mum and Dad.'

'Oh,' she replied, still looking uncertain.

'Shall I let them in?'

She shrugged. 'It's up to you.'

'They might have presents.'

'Do you want their presents?'

'Or money.'

'We don't need their money.'

'No, but we could take it and use it for something wasteful and indulgent.'

'Like what?'

'I don't know. Crack. Sex-toys.'

'Do you want crack or sex-toys?'

'No, not really. And they'd probably think that was cool anyway. But maybe we should let them in. It is Christmas.'

'You decide, Steve. I won't think any less of you either way.'

I took another look down at them. They hadn't rung the bell again and were standing waiting patiently for my response. I suddenly felt a wave of affection for them and decided to let them in.

'Hello, son,' smiled my father as I opened the door, 'it's been a while.'

'Yeah,' I replied, 'sorry about that.'

'No, no, don't worry,' he said, 'I know what it's like when you're in that first flush of love.'

'Oh, you do, do you?' my mother demanded. 'Who's this, then?'

'Why don't you come in?' I asked. 'Save you fighting on the doorstep.'

It wasn't surprising that Cherry hated my parents. Their first meeting had not gone well. I had made a more serious mistake than I realised by telling my Dad about the agency that had brought us together. He was still convinced it was some kind of con, arranged by criminals out to scam his inexperienced son. Mum knew nothing about Soumenda or Harry Hollingsworth; her objections to Cherry were entirely personal. I had assumed she'd be pleased I'd finally found a girlfriend, but now I wondered whether she preferred it when I was single and if this was a factor in why I'd taken so long to discover my ideal partner. I think what made my mother anxious (aside from the strange vibes from Dad) was that she could probably sense this one was serious, and she hadn't had a say in the selection. She would have been happiest, I believe, if I'd been a womaniser. I think she felt frustrated that she loved Dad so much, and wanted to be surrounded by the excitement of someone else's casual sex. But Cherry had to accept some of the blame for the uneasy relations, as she definitely disliked my parents. Which, as I said before, only made me love her more.

'So, have you been to a fancy dress party?'

Dad laughed and took off his comedy top hat. He put it down on the table. 'Just a bit of fun, son, that's all. Look,' he said, lifting up a plastic bag, 'we brought you presents.'

'Oh,' I said, 'I haven't got anything for you yet.'

'Yet?' demanded Mum. 'It's Christmas Day.'

'Don't worry about that, son,' Dad said. 'We don't need anything.'

Mum surveyed the remains of the Christmas dinner on the table. 'Did you do all this, Cherry? If that's what's left over it must have been a real feast. What am I saying? Of course you did it, my son doesn't know how to cook.'

'Would you like something?' Cherry asked. 'There's plenty of turkey, and bread for sandwiches.'

'No,' she said, 'that's OK, we had our own big lunch and with three days of leftovers in front of me I don't want to start just yet. Dennis, give them their presents.'

'All right,' he said, opening the bag and putting two boxes on the table. 'This one's for you, Steve.'

I unwrapped my present. It was a Sony DCR-TRV330 Digital 8 Camcorder.

'I remembered how much you liked that video camera I bought you when you were a teenager. This one is top-of-the-range: it plays Hi-8, 8mm, and, of course, you can feed it through your PC.'

My father waited for my response. I was touched and didn't know what to say. The video camera he'd bought me in 1987 had been my most prized possession until I sold it to supplement my student grant. I'd sold it a few weeks into term and always regretted that I hadn't kept it to shoot some footage of the women I'd slept with, especially after seeing *Sex, Lies and Videotape* in my second year. I don't mean that I want to produce amateur porn – I never want to witness myself having sex on screen – just something to help me remember them. Of course, if they'd let me record them undressing I wouldn't have complained, but that wasn't my main priority, and I'm sure most of the women would have felt excited and empowered by the experience. Having a camera now I had Cherry was unbearably exciting, and I couldn't wait to kick my parents out and start filming. It might have been a slightly smutty present – I had few illusions about what my parents would do with a digital camcorder – and this may have been why I felt estranged from them, but in my excitement all this was forgotten.

'Dad,' I said, 'thank you. I think this is the nicest Christmas present I've ever been given.'

He looked taken aback by this genuine display of emotion – rare from me – and started detailing all the camera's features. I let him continue but tuned out, and my mother said, 'Cherry, open your present.'

She picked up the package, excited by my gift and no doubt hoping hers was equally lavish. Cherry tore off the paper and the present tumbled out: a StyleSpa Deluxe Pedicure Kit. It was a sick joke, or would have been if my parents knew about the condition of Cherry's feet. As it was, it was simply an unfortunate coincidence, although Cherry reacted as if it was a deliberate trick.

'Oh,' she said, hurt, 'oh . . .'

'What's wrong?' Dad asked.

Cherry pulled off the bunched socks that covered the ends of her feet.

'Christ,' said Dad, horrified by the mess, 'what happened to you?'

She was sobbing too hard to respond. Mum looked at me, and I said, 'Thanks for the camera, Dad, but it might be best if you left us alone now. I'll call you tomorrow.'

Despite their protestations, I soon had them out of the house.

'It's OK,' I told Cherry, stroking her hair, 'really, it's OK. They didn't mean anything.'

But it was too late. That was the last time Cherry saw my parents.

TWENTY-FOUR

I once heard a song on the radio called *Four Hearts in a Can*. It was about four friends in a car, although the lyric, as far as I can remember, was disappointingly elusive. Music muscles into my life (this story, remember, started with a Sinatra song), but I rarely go in search of it. This particular synecdochic connection struck me as something that could be improved upon in prose (even before I knew I would write this account). More interesting to me, though less original, than four hearts in a can, was two hearts in a bed, encased within their bodies' fleshy forms. There are any number of lyric poems about a lover watching his beloved sleep, but far more romantic to me are those hours of shared slumber. Stories about certain celebrities or politicians enjoying improbable erotic connections fascinate everyone, but for me the interest lies in those two bodies being in the same place. Two hearts together. Always more interesting than one, but it takes physical failure to remind you of the miraculous nature of any union. When I was single it seemed amazing that this could ever happen. Forget true love: just the rituals necessary to bring any two bodies together. And here I find this image sliding away from me before I've managed to get what I wanted from it. Somewhere in these last few sentences the content of the paragraph has twisted and what I now find myself focusing on is that imperfection – the heart of this account – that I've always feared and should have under-stood the significance of when my only concern was skipping

CDs. Disintegration. Every night Cherry arose several times, to vomit. I told her to wake me if she was worried, and it was ages before she did, but when it happened she shook me from dreams to whisper a new horror, 'My sick, Steve. It's black.'

Soon Cherry was feeling so frail that she stopped going in to school. For the first few days, I stayed home to nurse her, but I was worried that Fred might get suspicious about my absence and decided I should go into school again. If I'd known what a terrible sign black vomit was – if I'd known what it meant – I would have insisted she went to the doctor, hell, to the hospital she should be in, but I didn't, and for some reason she refused to seek further medical attention. I knew there had to be a reason why Cherry stayed away from physicians, but no matter how hard I pressed she refused to tell me. I felt bad about leaving Cherry alone and by lunchtime I couldn't take it any more.

'Tom,' I said, 'I'm worried about Cherry. I'm going to go home. I'll be back in time for afternoon lessons.'

'OK,' he said. 'Don't worry, if you get back late I'll find some way of covering your classes.'

I thanked him and headed home. Cherry was lying outside the bathroom. She was naked and asleep. I worried she was dead. But when I leaned down beside her, she said, 'It's cooler here. Cool . . . that's all.'

'It's OK, Cherry, I understand.'

'I think I'm dying, Steve.'

'You're not dying, Cherry, I promise. But this is why you need to go to the doctor.'

'I'm not going again,' she said. 'Not after what they did to me before.'

'When? When you asked him about your feet?'

She shook her head. 'Long before that.'

I pulled her body against mine. 'Cherry, I'm scared. This is no time for secrets.'

'It's OK,' she said, opening her eyes. 'I'm feverish, I don't know what I'm saying. Look, there's something I need you to help me to do.'

'Anything.'

'You have to get me to my mother. She'll know what to do.'

'OK,' I said, 'I'll call a taxi.'

'No,' she replied, 'not all the way. It's too expensive.'

'Forget about money, Cherry. It doesn't matter. Not now. Besides, it won't cost that much.'

'No,' she repeated. 'We can get a taxi to Waterloo and a taxi from Surbiton to Chessington. But we should make that train journey. It's OK, it's overground, and only a few stops. We need to save our money.'

I gently lifted her face up so she could see mine. 'Cherry, I can get money. If that's what you're worried about . . . if that's why you're not going to hospital . . . my parents have savings. I've never asked them for anything.'

'Take me to Mum,' she said. 'I want her to know. And I want her to meet you.'

I brought Cherry's clothes and helped her get dressed. I called for a taxi and then phoned Tom Carson on his mobile, leaving a message asking him to explain my absence. The taxi arrived suspiciously early, but it wasn't the right time to interrogate the driver. Cherry seemed exhausted, and her body was wet with cold sweat. I asked her, 'What's your Mum's address?'

She shook her head and told the driver in a loud voice, 'Waterloo station.'

The driver nodded and set off. I didn't understand why Cherry was being so insistent and, although I respected her wishes, I worried about how I would get her through the train journey. She fell asleep within seconds, her hot face pressed against my suit jacket. The driver kept checking the rear-view mirror, eventually asking, 'She's not going to throw up, is she?'

'If she does, I'll pay the clean-up fee.'

'I don't care about the fucking fee, mate, I can't have my cab stinking of vomit.'

'I'm not going to throw up,' Cherry told him.

He stopped outside Waterloo station. I paid him and helped Cherry out of the cab. She winced as her feet hit the pavement. I put my arm around her shoulders and we hobbled up the steps.

'The Surbiton train's the right one,' she said, as we walked into the station. 'Look, there's one in three minutes.'

We found the right platform and boarded the train, which had arrived early. I helped Cherry into a seat and she slumped against the window.

'See,' she said, 'I did it.'

The carriage was empty. A half-eaten McDonald's Happy Meal was smeared across the floor and the smell of this discarded food remained strong. I worried that it would make Cherry sick, but she seemed to have recovered slightly since she'd been in the cab.

'Cherry,' I said, as the train pulled out of the station, 'I don't want you to have to carry on this charade when we get to your mother's house. Tell me your real name.'

She looked confused. 'My name is Cherry.'

The train passed through several deathly stations before we reached our stop. I felt glad my parents had always resisted leaving the city. My mother had never been that fond of my grandfather's house and if she had persuaded him to move it would probably have been to somewhere like Wimbledon or New Malden.

We caught a taxi from outside the station. Further into a scary suburbia that offered none of the smooth security of its American equivalent and instead made me think of sexual frustration and unsolved murders. Of course Cherry had been born here. It made perfect sense. This was where every interesting English person began. Lacking this spur, I had relaxed into complacency at an early age.

Twenty minutes later, we passed a large cement playground and a rank of shops. Cherry sat up and said, 'Next left.'

The driver nodded and took the turn.

'Just up ahead. Here. Yes, that's great. Thank you.'

I paid and then helped Cherry out of the cab. Resting on my arm, she slowly walked up to her front door and rang the bell. I could hear movement inside the house. Someone was coming to the door. It opened. A woman in her late fifties smiled and said in a delighted voice, 'Cherry!'

We went inside.

'Mum,' she said, 'this is Steve.'

She tutted. 'I know that. Who else would it be? Go into the lounge. Make yourselves comfortable. I'll put the kettle on.'

Cherry did as her mother instructed. I followed her and the two of us sat together on a brown, yellow and orange settee. There was a row of family photographs on the mantelpiece opposite us. I noted Cherry's graduation photograph and said, 'So this really is your house?'

She didn't reply. I wondered whether she'd known when she started this that it would lead back here. Her mother ducked back through the doorway and asked, 'What would you like to drink, Steve? Tea? Coffee?'

'Coffee, please. Black.'

She nodded and returned to the kitchen. Still staring at the mantelpiece, I noticed some circus photographs. I wanted to get up and examine them – see how the illusion had been achieved – but was worried about upsetting Cherry.

Her mother returned with three mugs. 'Steve,' she said, 'I know it can be embarrassing when you meet your girlfriend's mother for the first time and you don't know what to call her, so I want you to know that I'm a Ms, not a Mrs, Smith . . . unless there's a situation where it's important for people to know I'm a widow . . . and my Christian name is

Sandra. You can call me Sandra, but it's always Sandra, never Sandy, OK? It's not that I'm a particularly pedantic person, but before my husband died I was Sandy to everyone and then after his death, as a mark of respect, but also to symbolise how I've changed . . . Sandy, you see, died with Cedric.'

'Cedric the Strongman?' I asked.

'That's right,' she said, brightening, 'has Cherry told you about us? I wasn't sure if she would. She goes through funny phases, my daughter.'

'Mum,' said Cherry, her voice anguished.

'What?' she asked. 'I'm not embarrassing you, am I?'

'I don't think it's that,' I told her. 'Your daughter's very sick, Sandra. I thought you would know what to do.'

Sandra stared at me. The physical resemblance between mother and daughter was so strong that I knew they had to be genuine relations. But that didn't mean anything else was true, even Cherry's previous story about being a business employee of Harry Hollingsworth. Sandra seemed more like an actress than her daughter, or rather, more actressy, which probably simply meant she was worse at her job. Cherry's performance was one of vacancy, a femme fatale who gave away the bare minimum to maintain her mystique. The mother seemed more elaborate in her performance, inhabiting her character and presenting her in a heightened, expressionistic style. The question was, how would she respond to Cherry's illness? Would she stay in character, or would her concern prevent her from maintaining this illusion? Just how good an actress was she?

'What's wrong with you?' she asked.

'I think I'm dying, Mum.'

'Dying? Don't be ridiculous. What are your symptoms?'

She listed them, then showed her mother her toes. Sandra sat down alongside us, deflated, and then said, 'Steve, I'm going to have to ask you to leave. Cherry, you stay with me. I'm going to call Soumenda.'

TWENTY-FIVE

'And you left?' Judith asked me later that night.

'It seemed the best thing to do. All I care about is that Cherry . . . or whatever her name really is . . . gets proper medical attention. There's obviously something seriously wrong with her . . . she thinks she's dying . . . and I think the reason why she wouldn't let me take her to a hospital is that it would blow this whole game, which means I'm the one who's standing in the way of her getting well again.'

Judith nodded. 'I understand, Steve. But do you think these people are trustworthy? And do they really have Cherry's best interests at heart?'

After I'd left Cherry's house, I wandered the suburban streets for ages, trying to find a bus stop. There would be no taxis here, and I could hardly hitchhike. I knew I had to get back to my flat, and after I'd been there a while I found myself feeling agitated. For the first time in my life I felt like sharing my problems with someone, but didn't know whom to approach. I couldn't face telling my parents what had happened, but I needed to talk to someone who knew the truth about Cherry. Then I remembered Tom. Although I'd told him my story about Your Perfect Woman was a joke, I knew he didn't believe me and that he was likely to be sympathetic. But when I got to his house he was out drinking with some university friends. I was ready to leave, but Judith could see I was upset and told me to come inside.

'So what should I do?' I asked her.

'Do you remember the address?'

'Yes. I don't know exactly how to find it again, but I know the address.'

'OK. I've got a map. Let's go.'

'What about Tom? Won't he be worried if he comes back and you're not here?'

'He deserves to worry. I've worried enough.'

I stared at Judith, shocked. As far as I was aware, Tom and Judith had a perfect marriage and this was the first time she'd said a cross word about him. Maybe it was because he wasn't here.

'OK,' I said.

We walked out to the car.

It felt strange being in a car with Judith. I'd always felt shyly attracted to her, although I never would have had the courage to make a pass at her and would have been horrified if she made a pass at me. I suppose I liked her because she was kind to me. It was a maternal thing. Not my mother, of course, but maybe someone else's. There had been times, as a child, when other people's mothers had paid unusual attention to me. This made me feel good, but also scared, as their consideration forced me to reveal things I would have preferred to keep private. It was the same with Judith. She'd always been fascinated by me, and I could tell she was excited about this adventure. But I worried about getting her involved, and feared that something terrible might happen. Even if these anxieties were far-fetched, there was a normal series of realistic embarrassments that would inevitably precede any possible confrontation. Number one was that I was no good at map-reading.

'OK,' she said, 'I won't need directions for a while. But if you could look for the street on the map.'

This, I could do.

Maybe you think I sound too relaxed about these events. The only woman I'd ever loved had been taken away from me; I was heading towards a possible confrontation with sinister strangers accompanied by my only friend's wife, and yet all that worried me was having my general ineptitude exposed. All I can say in my defence is that everything I'd told Judith was true: my only concern was that Cherry wouldn't die, and I trusted that when she'd been made well she would return to me. If it had been solely up to me I wouldn't have returned to Cherry's mother's house, but Judith had made me nervous and I wanted to check they were looking after my lover properly.

We continued to drive. I balanced the map in my lap. Judith drove crouched up close to the steering-wheel, peering through the windscreen and pecking her head round in several different directions whenever she approached a turning. Driving for Judith seemed to require an immense amount of concentration and I felt reluctant to distract her by speaking. When she eventually turned to me for directions I was as useless as I'd predicted and she took the map from me and checked the final stage of the journey herself.

'OK,' she said as we entered Cherry's road, 'tell me where to stop.'

The house was in darkness. We walked up to the front door and rang the bell several times. There was no sound from inside.

'They're probably at the hospital,' I told her.

'Let's break in.'

I stared at her, aghast. 'Judith . . . I don't want to go to prison.'

'But you want to know what the full story is, don't you? There could be all sorts of secrets about Cherry . . . or whoever she is . . . inside this house. This is your chance to get to the bottom of the mystery.'

Cowardice kicked in. 'What if we're caught?'

'If they're at the hospital, and Cherry's as sick as you say she is, they won't be back for ages. And these houses are easy to break into. Check under the mat. They probably keep a key there. And I bet they don't even *have* a burglar alarm.'

I lifted up the doormat. No key. Judith didn't seem discouraged. 'Let's go round the back. The easiest way into a house is always through the back.'

'Judith, have you done this before? I thought you were a speech therapist, not a cat burglar.'

She laughed. 'There's a lot you don't know about me, Steve.'

Judith went round to the gate at the side of the house, unlatched it, and started making her way down to the garden. I followed her, worried that the next-door neighbours would notice us. The back garden was empty of furniture. Judith started checking under the flower pots, finally announcing triumphantly, 'Aha!'

I had a pain in my chest and was finding it hard to breathe. 'Judith . . . I just need to sit down for a minute . . . my heart . . .'

'What's wrong with you?'

'It happens sometimes. Just let me sit down. It will pass in a minute.'

'You don't have to go inside if you're scared. You can stay outside and keep watch.'

'It's OK. I'm not scared. Just give me a minute.'

She stopped talking and sat down beside me. Any guilt I'd had about getting her involved with this had disappeared when I realised just how much she was enjoying this. I tried to match my breathing with hers and pressed my hand against my heart.

'Judith,' I asked, 'is your marriage in trouble?'

'What makes you think that?'

'Earlier, when I came round. You said you'd been worried about Tom.'

'Oh,' she said, 'not about anything serious. It just annoys me sometimes that he's so relaxed. He's not nervous like me.'

'You're not nervous.'

She laughed. 'Not about things like this. Not about *action*. My problem is that I worry about, I don't know, metaphysical questions. I think it's because of the difference between our jobs. When we were younger being a teacher and being a speech therapist seemed like almost identical careers, but they're not. You must know what I mean, you're a teacher. Teaching is a long-term thing, like a soap opera. You see children grow and you have all these relationships and you don't know where they're going to take you. But being a speech therapist, it's about fixing people. You get someone, and as quickly as possible, you make them better. So you don't have this thing . . . this stress, this, I don't know, life that fills your mind and stops you asking questions.'

'I think you have a very romantic view of teaching. Education is constant frustration.'

'For you, maybe, not Tom. Now, how are you feeling? Are you ready to go inside?'

Judith slid the key into the lock, twisted it, and pushed the door. It was stiff, but opened into a kitchen. It was a normal suburban kitchen, except there was no kettle, no bottles, no food, nothing. She opened the cupboards. They were empty. I ran through into the lounge. Everything that was there earlier, the photos, the TV, even the settee, had gone. Someone had even torn the carpets from the floor, leaving dusty patches of black underlay.

'Steve,' said Judith, 'What's going on?'

The telephone rang.

TWENTY-SIX

'Mr Ellis. You do realise you're trespassing?'

It was Soumenda. His voice, as always, was calm, unhurried, and far too confident for the job he had been given.

'All I care about is Cherry. That's all. Just tell me you got her to a hospital and she's OK.'

'We got her to a hospital. But she's not OK. At the moment she's in intensive care. You should have contacted us earlier, Mr Ellis.'

'I wanted to. I told Cherry we should. But I think she was scared.'

'Scared. Of what?'

'Of you. Of spoiling this scam. Whatever it's about . . .'

'Mr Ellis, please relax. You don't want to aggravate your heart condition.'

'I don't have a heart condition.'

'You don't?' he said, surprised. 'It runs in your family, doesn't it?'

'What makes you think that?'

'Your grandfathers . . . on both sides, I believe, as well as a great uncle. In fact, given your diet and the fact that the closest you come to exercise is filling in for a sick teacher for the occasional PE lesson, which you're uniquely unsuited to, not even owning a tracksuit or a pair of trainers, I wouldn't be surprised if when it does come to your turn to die, it turns out to be a heart attack.'

This was the closest he'd come to intimidating me, and I wondered whether Cherry's sickness had interfered with their plan. 'Soumenda, I just want Cherry to be OK. If there's something I can do for you, or Mr Hollingsworth.'

He drew breath. 'Mr Ellis, you are, I'm sure, aware of those free CD-Roms that are posted by internet providers to people's homes?'

'Yes.'

'In a week's time you will receive a CD that appears to be from an internet provider. This CD will not be from an internet provider. It will be from us. You have to put this CD not into your computer, but into your CD player. When you play the CD you will hear a message from us that will give you a series of instructions. If you successfully complete your first task, you will be given your second. Complete the second task to our satisfaction and Cherry will be returned to you, happy and healthy. Fail and not only will you never see her again, but we will . . . how should I put this . . . allow her to die.'

'Her sickness? Is it real? Is it something you've done to her?'

Soumenda chuckled. 'Let's just say she has a rare condition. Like your heart complaint. No one's to blame. Except God, of course, or if you'd prefer, your genes. Do you remember what Mr Hollingsworth told you the first time you met? A little indelicately expressed . . . but a perfect clue as to what would come. Cherry, like you, has been fucked in the arse by her family history. Or, maybe, in this case, family isn't the right word. But, don't worry, we can still save her, provided you do as you're told.'

'I checked in all the medical textbooks. Cherry's condition doesn't exist. You did something to her, didn't you? Some sort of poison . . . or . . . was the whole thing a fiction? Make up?'

'Very inventive, Mr Ellis. Even if you were on the right track you've got a lot of things muddled up. Far too inventive for us. Things are always a lot simpler than they first appear. And you're not a doctor, I believe I'm correct in saying? So I really don't think your diagnosis holds much water. Goodnight, Mr Ellis. You have two minutes to leave this house.'

'And after that?'

'I really don't think you want to find out. We may need you, but Mrs Carson is expendable. Two minutes.'

One minute later we were back in the car. I pulled my seatbelt around me and Judith started the engine.

'They really threatened to kill me?' she asked.

'Yes.'

'Just for breaking into their house? Wow.'

This was the only part of my conversation with Soumenda that I was going to share with Judith. I didn't want her to know that they wanted me to do something for them because I was sure that if she did she would stop me and I couldn't risk that. I was prepared to do anything to save Cherry's life.

Anything.

PART SIX

TWENTY-SEVEN

Our post usually arrives at midday. It would have been possible to return from school at lunchtime, but I was so anxious about getting hold of the CD, and what might be on it, that I took the day off. I came downstairs at 11.45 and waited in the hallway, grabbing the post the moment it came through the letterbox.

The CD wasn't there. I opened the door and chased after the postman. He was in his late fifties, with a grumpy face and curly ginger hair.

'If your cheque's not there it's not my fault. I can only deliver what comes in.'

'No, no, it's not a cheque. It's a CD.'

'Amazon?' he asked. 'When did they say it would come?'

'No, not Amazon. Not a music CD, actually. A CD-Rom. A 100-hour trial.'

'Those free things? You can get them from computer shops. Dixons.'

'I ordered one. A special one. From Harry Hollingsworth.'

'Who? Look, I'm sorry, mate. Besides, perhaps they're delivering it separately.'

He turned round and carried on down the road. The postman had a point. Perhaps the CD would be delivered later. Or perhaps it had already arrived.

'Yeah,' said the blond-haired student from downstairs, 'I took the CD. But what are you worried about? It's only a free trial.'

147

'But it was addressed to me.'

'I didn't know you wanted it. I get sent them all the time. I only grabbed that one because it was there on the mat and I needed to reboot my system. Some nasty fucker sent me a terrible virus.'

'Do you still have it?'

'The CD? Yeah, but I don't know why you're so worried about this particular one. It doesn't even work.'

'It's for special systems,' I said, 'that's why I need it.'

'Really?' he asked. 'It doesn't say that on the packet.'

'No, I know. Look, it's really important. Can you please get it for me?'

The student nodded, turned round and went back inside his flat. He left the door open but I didn't follow him. I could see one of the dark-haired female students down inside the flat, standing in the kitchen eating a bowl of cornflakes by the sink. She was wearing a blue silk dressing-gown. I smiled at her and she waved at me, flexing a foot against the dirty brown floor.

'Here you go,' said the student, handing the CD back to me. 'What system is it for?'

'I don't know anything about computers,' I told him. 'It's for my system. That's all I know.'

He nodded and scratched his chin. 'Do you know what's happening with Mr Butler, by the way? That mad swearing bloke hasn't been around in ages.'

'I came to a settlement with him.'

'Really?' the student asked. 'How much did you get?'

'Nothing. He just fixed my ceiling and let me off some of the rent.'

'Let you off the rent? Shit, I could do with that. Hey, by the way, we're having a party on Friday. If it's too noisy just bang on the ceiling and we'll turn the music down.'

'OK,' I said, 'thanks.'

*

I ran upstairs and opened the door. Walking across to my CX110, I opened the top-loading system and slid the CD inside. I turned the volume up, and sat opposite the stereo, my mouth open as I waited to hear my instructions.

There was silence for a moment, and I worried that the student had given me the wrong CD. But then a voice came through the speakers.

'Hello, Steven, this is Harry Hollingsworth. I'm sorry about the way things have worked out. You seemed a truly genuine bloke when I met you and all I really wanted to do was help you out. I'm closer to Cherry than anyone else in the world . . . except you, by the sound of it, but even you haven't spent as much time with her as I have. I'm sorry that we have to threaten you, and to be honest, it would be very hard for me to cause Cherry any pain, and the only reason I'm making these threats is because I know you're going to come through for me. You don't know anything about me, Steve. Everything anyone has told you about me is a lie. The truth is I'm a very good person. Probably one of the very few genuinely good people out there. Because to be good, to be truly good, you have to have the power to do evil. What I'm saying is good has to be a conscious choice. But you also have to have money. True evil can only really be achieved with time and money. Lots of money. I'm talking evil on a grand scale. Evil on a scale even our world leaders couldn't imagine. And because I'm a good person I am able to operate outside of conventional morality and conventional law. Obviously it is difficult for me to ask you to do this . . . what am I saying? It's not difficult for me at all. But it's difficult for you to believe me, and to believe that you will be protected. You have to trust me, and given what I've done to you so far, that's an unfair thing to ask.

'I have had not unlimited, but considerable wealth, for an incredibly long time. OK, I'll come clean, it's family money. No doubt, for someone on a teacher's salary, it's hard to believe that a life with money could present any difficulty at all, but it does, Steve, it does. I'm not saying my life is any less difficult than yours, but I am presented with the problem of how to utilise my assets in a way that will create good in our world. Let me tell you a story. You remember the first time we met, when I told you that 1947 was my favourite year, because I turned seventeen? Well, that was true, but what I didn't tell you was that 1947 was my favourite year because it was the last year before I lost my innocence. In 1948, my father subjected me to a series of challenges. These challenges were a test of character. Most of the challenges were to do with questions of good and evil. He put me in a situation where I had to kill a man, where I had to choose between two men I didn't know and decide which one of them deserved to die. You may believe that no one deserves to die, but they do, Steve, they do.

'Your friend, Tom Carson, deserves to die. Tom Carson is the latest alias of a man who prefers to be known as the Fox. No doubt this sounds ludicrous to you. People with criminal connections, people who have committed enormous atrocities in the name of what they believe to be right do not work as teachers in comprehensive schools. But Tom Carson does. I know that Tom Carson deserves to die because Tom Carson used to be on my payroll. And there was a time when Tom Carson was a force for good. But all that was over a long time ago. I'm not going to tell you about Tom Carson's connections, who he works for, what he believes, because this should not be a question of ideology, it should be a question of trust. I'm asking you to commit a murder for me. I am asking you to remove a force of evil from the world. If you trust me, you will kill Tom Carson. If you don't, Cherry will die. It's as simple as that. Do it my way and a good person lives and an evil person dies. Refuse or resist, and the situation is reversed. Can you live with that, Steve Ellis? I don't know if I can.

'Stop the CD now. This is the end of track one. When you've had time to digest this information come back and start the CD again with track two. On the rest of this CD you will find advice on how to kill a man without drawing attention to yourself. Don't worry, you don't have to do it now. You will have plenty of time to train. And then, the moment you will kill the Fox will be when the two of you go to Paris together. If you do this, you will stop him attending an important meeting and you will save hundreds of lives. That's worth killing a man for, isn't it, Steve. Surely you've read Bentham, or seen *Star Trek*, an educated man like you? The needs of the many, always, always, outweigh the needs of the few. Or what about your Isaiah Berlin? Remember, Steve, the fox may know many things, but the hedgehog knows one big thing. You're my hedgehog and the big thing you know is that you're acting as a force for good. It has to be like that. You understand, don't you, Steve? I hope so.'

Oddly, given all that happened afterwards, my first reaction after hearing the CD was to return to school. In a way, it was a relief. I now knew what I had to do to get Cherry back. Or, rather, the first thing. If this was the warm-up, who knew what was going to follow?

I got back to school in time for the afternoon lessons. When Cherry had first fallen ill, the headmaster had asked me to take over the teaching of her Religious Studies lessons. I knew nothing about theology but, as Fred Lane pointed out, neither did most supply teachers. I had Cherry's notes and textbooks, and as any teacher will tell you, it's not hard to bluff an underage audience, even a small A-Level group. Most students get through school without cracking a spine. They might be prepared to read stuff on the internet, but usually no more than a few sentences to check they're downloading the right essay before changing the font and handing it in.

The five students in Cherry's class were pleasant company, easy-going and all vaguely amazed that RS lessons were merely formal versions of the stoned debates they had at house parties or in the backrooms of nightclubs at the weekend. At first they'd been sad to lose Cherry, but they seemed to have adjusted. In fact, they now liked me more, as the pace of my classes was slower and I was more indulgent of their sillier theories. I knew this because they told me. They were a remarkably guileless and open group.

I got up from behind my desk and wrote 'THEODICY' on the blackboard in blue chalk. The three girls sat up, wondering whether they were actually going to learn something today.

'What does that mean, Steve?' Alison asked.

'Does anyone know?'

No answer.

'Theodicy is a word that is believed to have been coined by a German mathematician and scientist called Gottfried Leibnitz. The word is derived from the Greek words *theos*, meaning God, and *dike*, meaning justice. Leibnitz believed there was a reason for everything that exists in our world. He also believed, and you'll remember this was something we talked about in our lesson on "Arguments for the Existence of God", that the ultimate reason for everything that exists in our world is God. He believed that our world was the most perfect of all possible worlds, and that because we only observe the world in parts we do not understand that everything that exists has to exist in order to create the most perfect world. Therefore, Leibnitz argued, evil was a necessary part of the most perfect world, and served the greater good.'

'Is this to do with utilitarianism?' Mark asked, and I shivered, realising I wasn't going to be able to get through this lesson without thinking of Harry Hollingsworth.

'No,' I said, 'not directly. Leibnitz wasn't . . .' here I had no idea whether I was misrepresenting the long dead thinker '. . . very clear on the question of human culpability. I think he saw sin as something that happened to people rather than an active thing. So it wasn't a question of making a moral choice. But let me be a bit more specific about what today's lesson is about. I am not concerned with the bad things that happen in the world, like disease . . .'

Two students exchanged glances. They clearly believed I was talking about Cherry, and gave me sympathetic looks. I ignored them, knowing that allowing myself to think about her would make me cry.

'No,' I said, 'what we're discussing today is the question of human evil. Bad people doing bad things. Of course a lot of Christians would see this being better defined as sin . . .'

I was steering into safer waters. The recording of Harry Hollingsworth repeated in my mind, but as I stopped lecturing my students and allowed them to prattle on, it was possible to forget that this wasn't a theoretical conversation and that I faced a chilling ethical quandary of my own. I ended the lesson almost convinced that I would find another answer and get Cherry back without taking another man's life.

TWENTY-EIGHT

The following Friday Tom and Judith invited me to dinner. I had been spending a lot of time with my friend, desperate for some evidence that Harry Hollingsworth's accusations were true. But even if I knew Tom Carson was a murderer, would that make it any easier for me to execute him? I had put off listening to the rest of the CD, knowing that there were still two weeks before the Paris trip and still praying something might change before then.

Tom and Judith hadn't invited anyone else this evening. Judith was desperate to hear the latest developments in the Cherry situation and knew I wouldn't be prepared to talk about it if there was anyone else, besides Tom, in the room. Tom and I drove over to his house together after school. We were having a conversation about our classes and students and I asked, 'Tom, do you think murder can ever be justified?'

The words sounded so blunt spoken aloud. He kept his eyes on the road but there was concern in his voice as he asked, 'Is this about Cherry?'

'No, it's just a theoretical question. I was interested . . . it came up today in my RS lesson.'

He relaxed. 'Well, the one my students always like is killing Hitler. You know, if you could go back in time to when he was still a frustrated painter and take him out, would you do it? It's hard to see how that could be considered wrong, apart from changing the course of history. But that's not what you're asking, is it? If you're asking on a personal level, well, as you know, I'm no wishy-washy liberal. In the majority of cases, I'm pro-war and I think there are very few good politicians who don't have some blood on their hands.'

I watched Tom, wondering if this answer revealed anything. 'War is different. What I'm asking you is: would you kill if you believed in the cause?'

'You mean if I went to war?'

'No. If, say, you knew I was an evil, dangerous person would you kill me? If you had the chance?'

'You're not an evil person, Steve.'

'I know, but if I was . . . Can you imagine ever killing another human being?'

'Truthfully?'

'Of course.'

'If someone did something to Judith, I would have no problem tracking them down and killing them. But I think even in that case I would prefer to let the police handle it. If, after pursuing all the proper legal channels, the person wasn't sentenced or got out after six months, I believe, if Judith wanted me to, I would be prepared to kill them.'

I was glad we were having this conversation in a car. Tom was a much more relaxed driver than his wife, but he still needed to watch the road and that stopped him looking at me and guessing what I was thinking. He didn't seem to be waiting for me to answer so I kept quiet, unable to change the subject. We stopped off at an off-licence. I handed him a twenty-pound note.

'Choose a bottle of wine for me. You know what to buy.'

Tom nodded and left me alone in the car. I waited until he entered the off-licence and then opened the glove compartment. There was nothing incriminating inside, just a map, a couple of compilation tapes and a tin of barley sugar. I quickly closed it back up and waited for Tom to return.

'Dead Arm,' he said as he got back in the car.

'What?'

'The wine. I hope that's OK. I thought it was best to go expensive tonight. Don't worry, I've paid the extra. Quality, not quantity. I have a couple of bottles of plonk at the house if this turns into a proper session.'

Tom unlocked his front door and we went inside. Judith hadn't dressed up in the way she usually did for her dinner parties. She was sitting watching a soap-opera on a television in the lounge. As we entered the lounge she got up and went across to turn it off. Tom kissed her on the lips and then she kissed me on both cheeks.

'So,' asked Judith, 'any news?'

I remembered my story. 'Nothing new. Soumenda calls me every evening and gives me an update . . .'

'This is the man who threatened to kill me?' she said excitedly.

'Yes. Cherry's out of intensive care, but she still needs constant supervision.'

Tom went out into the kitchen for a corkscrew. Judith grinned at me. Since our adventure she had become even more conspiratorial with me, which I could tell had started to annoy Tom.

'How long until dinner's ready?' he asked Judith.

'Twenty minutes. But the starter's done. Shall we sit at the table?'

We did so. Judith went out to the kitchen. Tom took two glasses and said, 'I really should decant this wine and let it stand for a while, but I can't be bothered to wait. Now, Steve, this is a very rich, heavy wine, so if you're not familiar with it take it slowly.'

He was talking to me as if I was one of his students. We all did this sometimes, an inevitable effect of talking down to others all day. 'OK,' I replied.

Judith returned with three bowls of duck salad and placed them in front of us. Tom filled my glass with wine. I made a big show of appreciating the drink before taking a swallow, then made it look as if I was really savouring it, even though it tasted disgusting.

'So,' asked Judith, 'have you seen her?'

'No, they won't tell me where she is.'

'Steve, I don't want to upset you, but don't you think it might be better to sever your ties with these people? I know you love Cherry, but she clearly isn't the woman you think she is . . .'

Tom touched his wife's arm, warning her that she was about to go too far. I slowly chewed my food, trying to control my temper. 'I know Cherry,' I said. 'It doesn't matter what her real name is . . . if she was called Chloë or Tracey or Becca or Diana it wouldn't make any difference, it wouldn't change how I felt about her. It's like falling in love with an actress. The character the actress is playing might be different from the actual person, but you still love the actress for the person, not the character.'

'That doesn't make that much sense, Steve.'

'Yes, it does,' I said, 'and anyway, Cherry never lies.'

'What does that mean?'

'She told me. She never lies.'

Tom and Judith exchanged looks. She was the one who spoke first, saying slowly, 'I think only a liar would swear to something like that. Steve, there are some things we have to say to you. I know you hate confrontation, and I don't like to do this, but you don't seem to have that many other friends who care about you, and I know you have a strange situation with your parents. I believe these people are using you. I'm not sure why, and I'm not sure what they want you to do, but this is definitely a scam of some sort. I assumed they wanted you to marry Cherry, but I didn't know why. You're not wealthy, and she's English, so the obvious reasons are ruled out. Now I think there is something more sinister at work here. They've clearly picked on you because you have low self-esteem . . .'

'I don't have low self-esteem.'

'Steve, don't you realise how attractive you are? You're much more attractive than Cherry. You've let yourself go a bit, sure, but the raw material ... my God, you're an incredibly handsome man. Why do you think I kept trying to fix you up with my friends? I wasn't doing that out of charity. If you had opened up, just one tiny bit, any of those women would have been happy to go home with you. This old man you met, Harry Hollingsworth, he clearly spotted the sucker in you and now they're playing you for all you're worth. You have to call an end to this, Steve. You're the only one who can do it.'

I remained calm. 'Judith, if what you were saying was true, don't you think they would have already asked me to do something? I admit that it's strange, but I'm sure it's something whimsical rather than evil. Harry's playing a game of some sort ... a rich man's folly ... I know that. But I also think that there's nothing sinister behind it. She's probably his niece or something. Cherry's a playful sort too. It's just a wheeze they've cooked up together. And I'm sure the sickness isn't part of it.'

'What about the man who tried to kill me?'

'I made that up.'

'What?'

'You were getting so into it. I wanted to make it fun for you.'

They both looked at me with a look that suggested they weren't sure if this was true, but even if it was, it would only make them more worried about me. Still, the lie served its purpose and ended the conversation. After a short period of silence, we started talking about the Paris trip instead. I could tell their concern had changed to irritation, and after the coffee I asked them to order me a taxi. Judith walked me to the door, where she gripped my arm and whispered, 'If you want to talk to me when Tom's not here, just call, OK?'

I nodded, and went out to the cab.

I still had Cherry's possessions. Of all the strange things that had happened, this struck me as the strangest. What woman, no matter how sick, could do without everything she'd ever owned? This should have been reassuring. It wasn't. I sensed that Soumenda and Harry Hollingsworth were staying away from me, but it would have been easy for them to break in while I was out. For the first few nights after she'd gone, I'd left Cherry's clothes in the wardrobe, but then I'd found myself unable to sleep and decided to make a Cherry doll out of two pillows. I dressed the top pillow in the blue denim jacket and white top she'd been wearing when we first met, the bottom pillow in her black skirt. It was incredibly comforting holding this pillowbody, and I soon managed to drift off. The next night I wore these clothes myself, stretching a pair of her dirty knickers over my face, mouth lipsticked with her lipstick, and masturbated so that my ejaculate – saved up since she'd gone – shot all over her top. I found bloody cotton wool pads that had been pressed onto her toes and ate them all. I knew she would understand when she returned. Tonight I pushed my cock inside one of her boots and rubbed until I came. When I pulled my cock out it was bloody and black from the inside of the boot. I knew it would hurt in the morning, but I also knew I would sleep.

TWENTY-NINE

When I woke up, Len was standing in my bedroom. I didn't scream, but I did wince as my raw penis rubbed against the duvet.

'You should never have given them a key. That's where you went wrong.'

'Len, what's all this about?'

He sat down on the edge of my bed. 'Magic doesn't exist. It's just a question of controlling other people's perceptions. You do know they all know each other, don't you? Butler, Hollingsworth, Soumenda . . . not that he's who he seems to be either, I'm afraid.'

I noticed Len had stopped swearing. This frightened me more than the fact that he was inside my flat. After all, he'd performed that trick before.

'Know how to make money? Sell people what they want. And if you don't have anything people want? Pay money to someone to make people think they want what you have. But even this won't work if you don't have a clear idea of who your customer is going to be. It used to be so much easier in my day. You were defined by what you dealt in. Or further back, when you were named for your trade. Cherry is a beautiful woman. You chose well. She's trustworthy too. Her getting sick *was* part of the scam, but it was something that was done to her, if you see what I mean. She didn't want to go through with it. She thought she was strong. Stronger than them. But she will survive . . . if you do this one small thing, and one other, more distasteful, but easier, requiring less effort . . . and she will return to you.'

Len took off his glasses. His eyes still bulged, unmagnified but just as frightening. When he spoke again, it was in a quieter voice. 'Steve, say Cherry hadn't lived up to your expectations, if they'd ignored the specifications, if she'd been blonde instead of brunette, what would you have done?'

'That wouldn't have happened, Len. Cherry told me herself. She said that she worked for Harry Hollingsworth and was chosen because she fitted my description of the perfect woman. Harry must know hundreds of women, it could have been any one of them.'

Len laughed. 'It's interesting, what you choose to believe. We all do it, of course, otherwise we'd be paranoid lunatics. But the way you select bits of information and fix on them as the truth . . .' He shook his head. 'What if I was to tell you that Cherry's a blonde, that she dyes her hair?'

'I know that's not true.'

'Why? Because her collar matches her cuffs? Her carpet her curtains? That doesn't prove anything. Do you like those phrases, by the way? Very Len, aren't they? Although he'd probably say something even more graphic.' He put his glasses back on. 'There are cameras in this room, do you know that? Brian put them in before Cherry arrived. That day you came home and wanted to have sex with Cherry in the hallway, he was checking everything worked. If you want proof, then let's just say I know why you're wincing this morning. But that's not important. I'm here for a reason. You haven't been listening to your CD, you haven't been training. Mr Hollingsworth wants this done properly, and it's not easy to kill a man, undetected. I'll wait in the lounge while you get dressed.'

I could have kicked him out, but that would only have created more trouble. Instead, I got out of bed, got dressed and went into the lounge. Len presented me with a knife, we up-ended my settee, and then spent most of the day working on manoeuvres. Soon Len and I both got so sweaty that we stripped to our trousers and shoes, practising grappling and working out what I would do if things went wrong and Tom attacked me back. The physical exertion was something of a relief, and although I flinched when Len first touched my body, I soon wanted to impress him and found a surprising strength. Violence proved much easier than I'd imagined, and I realised this was something that had always been in me. I thought back to when I grabbed that student who insulted Cherry and realised how close I'd come to really hurting him. I had a motivation for killing Tom: I wanted Cherry back. But I needed to get beyond seeing him as a normal human being. Len tried to banish my squeamishness by saying I should think it was Tom who had taken Cherry away from me. When that didn't work, he said that he had a video recording of Tom having sex with Cherry. I was about to throttle him, when he quickly added, 'That's not true, of course, I'm just trying to psyche you up. But that's what you should tell yourself. Imagine Tom fucking Cherry just before you do it.'

'OK,' I said, 'that'll work. But I can't take any more of this today, Len, OK? I need you to give me some time alone.'

'I respect that,' he said. 'Listen to that CD as often as you can. And train. All day tomorrow, at the very least. If you do that, I think you'll soon be ready. OK, Steve?'

I nodded.

After Len had gone, I put the settee back down and collapsed into it. I was in so much pain. My raw penis, my aching muscles: all these twinges combined and left me in a shivering warmth that felt oddly feminine. It was a strange kind of sensitivity that is hard to explain. The immediate reason for making this connection was, of course, Cherry, who had been in such agony almost from the moment we met. But other women I'd known (my mother, girls at uni) seemed to exist in a physical realm different from the one I lived in. Every time I bought new shoes and they rubbed my feet, it unleashed a feeling in me that I understood as female. It was a sense that pain is a constant part of life, something to be survived without complaint. Period pain. The pain of pregnancy. Childbirth. Those initial afflictions that Cherry suffered. My pain, though trivial, made me feel close to her.

Cherry, don't worry, we'll soon be together again.

PART SEVEN

THIRTY

There were eighteen students in the French A-Level group. We'd told them to assemble outside Victoria Coach Station at six am. This was Tom's idea, but I don't think he realised how busy it would be, even at this hour. Neither of us had met most of this group before, so I was relieved to see Alison from my RS group. She could help us find the others and prevent them from boarding the wrong coach.

In order to get to the station for six, I'd had to get up at five, and I was still feeling sleepy and sick. I hate travelling, and don't understand why something supposed to appeal to the civilised mind is geared around rising early. I'd expected Tom to have no problem with being up at this hour, but he looked as bleary-eyed as I did, and I realised it was safer to put Alison in charge.

Victoria Station is an unpleasant place to be at any time, but this morning it seemed especially grim, as packed with pensioners as a post office, and filled with the sickening stench of diesel. Alison dropped her backpack and started running back and forth, gathering students. A surprising number were dropped off by their parents. The idea of anyone who went to our school having a fully functional family astonished me, and I wondered which two students had enjoyed the dubious benefits of physical congress with Lafont and Lalande, the last two people I'd trust to act *in loco parentis*.

Soon we had fifteen students. Tom and I found our coach.

The driver was sitting behind the steering wheel, smoking a cigarette. We knocked on the windscreen, but he ignored us until he'd finished his fag, then the door slid out and open with a sudden whoosh. Alison returned with the remainder of our group and we all filed inside.

'That everyone?' the driver asked.

Tom nodded. The two of us took the traditional teachers' seats at the front of the coach. I sat behind the driver. He was in his fifties or sixties with thick strands of grey and white hair pasted down from the back of his shiny bald head. He launched into motion, starting the engine and manoeuvring the coach out of the station.

I leaned against the window. Tom stood up, took off his jacket and folded it into the luggage rack above the seats. He was wearing a white shirt and a red tie. The students seemed to be settling down, and the driver turned on the stereo, although at an almost inaudible volume. I can never sleep on any form of transport, no matter how tired I am. Travel simply makes me too nervous.

I wasn't thinking about what I had been instructed to do to Tom. Len had told me that if I was going to use a weapon I'd have to buy it in France, although he encouraged me to do the deed with my hands. He'd given me a pair of gloves and they were sitting in my bag, but apart from that I had made no further preparation. This had to be the least premeditated premeditated murder ever.

The journey was so boring that I did a totally unnecessary headcount and then went round taking everyone's name. Tom managed to make his newspaper last for ages, but after he'd finished it the two of us were reduced to staring out of the window.

Clacket Lane Service Station came as a huge relief.

'Fifteen minutes,' the driver told us.

The next leg of the journey passed more quickly, thanks to the copies of *GQ* and *Force* I'd bought at the service station.

Reading on coaches usually makes me feel sick, but because I wasn't paying much attention to the articles it didn't affect me today. Some of the photographs in *Force* were so explicit that I worried one of the students might think I'd bought pornography and report me. I was pleased when Tom asked to borrow it, thinking I could always pretend the magazine was his. But before I passed it over, I noticed a special travel supplement in the centre pages, providing a guide to S&M clubs around the world. I thumbed through until I found Paris, and then looked for one near the third arrondissement.

When we reached Dover, the coach driver alighted from the vehicle and went over to one of the cubicles to pay and get a time for the train that would transport coach, students and teachers to Calais. Ten minutes later we went through a small gate, stopped at immigration control and all the students had to hold up their passports to the window before we were allowed to pass through.

There wasn't too much of a delay and we soon joined the queue waiting for the next train. We inched forward slowly and eventually reached the ramp that led down into a flattened carriage. There were no sides to the carriage, but when we drove onto it, concertinaed walls rose up and sealed us in. I peered through the windscreen. There was an airlock between each coach area, and the driver told us if we wanted to stretch our legs during the short journey, it was possible to move between carriages. The students were eager to get out of the coach but, for the moment, Tom and I stayed in our seats. One of the students stopped and asked Tom, 'How come we can't see any fishes?'

The driver, overhearing, laughed. 'If we see fishes, we're in trouble.'

Towards the end of the crossing, the driver told me, 'You should go and round them up.'

'OK,' I replied, getting off the coach. Once I left our carriage, every single space seemed to be filled with students, and it was impossible to tell which were ours. I was relieved when I found Alison and delegated my duty. Before she set off, she asked, 'What's that boy doing?'

I turned round. A dark-haired teenager was attempting to dismantle one of the doors, using a knife as a screwdriver.

'I'll sort him out,' I told her, 'go and get the others.'

Alison turned and ran off. I approached the teenager, palms outstretched. 'What are you doing?'

The teenager muttered something in French. I pointed at his knife and then held out my hand. He seemed to consider arguing, dismissed the idea, and gave me the knife. I folded the blade away and put it in my back pocket. Although I have no French, I recognised the swearword he hissed at me as soon as my back was turned.

When I was back on the coach, I walked down the aisle to an empty double seat and, after making sure no one was watching me, slid the knife down a gap in the seat. It seemed that getting a weapon into the country was going to be remarkably easy.

THIRTY-ONE

Mme Lalande and M. Lafont had proved good sports about being prevented from going on the Paris trip. I think they were scared about the possible scandal and grateful to the headmaster for hushing it up. I'd never had much time for M. Lafont, but he had handed me a surprisingly jovial set of instructions and recommendations for the trip. There was no firm itinerary, but at some point over the next two days he suggested that we take the students up the Eiffel Tower (third level optional, depending on how scared they seemed), to the Sacré-Coeur and the Pompidou Centre, and on a journey down the Seine. The most important thing, he said, was to decide how much freedom to give them (MAXIMUM FREE-DOM, he recommended in bold blue biro, as well he might) and to find somewhere safe to lose the students so you could have a decent dinner. He suggested one of Montmartre's parks, or the Lafayette shopping centre as the safest place to abandon them, and then gave us a list of personally recommended restaurants and bars. Tom was less amused by his instructions than me, and suggested that for the first night at least we should eat dinner with the students. This meant going somewhere cheaper than Tom would have pre-ferred, so as not to stretch the students' limited funds, but he thought it would be best if we made an effort at the beginning and then gave them greater freedom as we went on.

Tom seemed less comfortable in France than I'd assumed

he would be. His ease around food and wine, as well as his general confidence in any situation, made me think he would be a fluent French speaker, but although he seemed to have the basics of the language he quickly switched to English in any prolonged conversation with French people we encountered, and if they didn't understand he sent Alison forward with instructions instead.

Alison was proving to be extremely useful. The rest of the group seemed more intimidated by her than they were by us, and often looked to her for approval before saying anything. The restaurant we went to was more of a bar, with cheap, grotty food. There were long tables and almost all the students managed to squeeze together onto the same one. Tom, Alison, a male student called Jason and I sat together on a separate square table away from the others. We ordered food and I asked Alison, 'Who's the student who's been shagging M. Lafont?'

She stared down at the table. Tom gave me an angry look.

'Shit,' I said, 'sorry.' I turned to Jason. 'And are you the male student?'

Jason stared back at me. 'What male student?'

'Nothing, never mind. I'm sorry, Alison.'

It hadn't occurred to me that she might be the student in question. For some reason, I assumed that someone as sensible as Alison wouldn't be interested in sexual relations with her teacher. She was just too clever and nice. The girls that I imagined slept with their teachers were the ones I sometimes taught who could hardly breathe without flirting. The predatory, scary students. Students whom stories circulated about. But then I remembered Fred Lane telling me that the girl who slept with M. Lafont was one of the school's only high-fliers. In the short time I'd spent with Alison, I could see how that could be true.

After dinner, Tom turned his chair round so he was facing the table of students and said, 'OK, you all know where the hotel is. You can do whatever you want tonight, but try not to go crazy. There's two more days to go, and we're going to have a busy day tomorrow. If you're going to go to a nightclub or a bar, go in pairs, and remember that drinks in some of these places can be extortionately expensive. Steve and I are going to return to the hotel. We'll be having a drink in the bar and then going to bed. If anyone wants to come with us, you're more than welcome.'

Unsurprisingly, none of the students, not even Alison, wanted to come back to the hotel with us. Tom and I walked back slowly through the Paris streets, enjoying the space and the darkness. Our hotel was one of those establishments I assume must be popular in France, which are more like houses than hotels (although infinitely more appealing than the English guest house). It reminded me of my parents' house, and there was even a large chimney my father would have enjoyed sitting alongside. The small bar area was like someone's lounge with a few extra tables. It was empty. Tom and I sat together and he went up to the bar, returning with two bottled beers and tall glasses. I poured my beer into my glass and said to him, 'I'm sorry about saying that thing to Alison.'

He laughed. 'That's OK. I was just surprised you hadn't already worked it out.'

'Could you ever do it?'

'Sleep with Alison? She's not really my type. She's got really stringy hair.'

'No,' I said, 'I mean with any of them.'

He sipped his beer and stared at me. 'Could you?'

'Tom, I was single for twelve years. If I was going to sleep with a student I would have done it a long time ago.'

'We used to think you did. Judith and me. You were single for so long and always freaked out when she tried to fix you up. We were convinced, for a while, that schoolgirls were your thing. We thought that either you did it and were so clever at picking out discreet girls that no rumours ever emerged, or maybe that you were one of those types who never lay a hand on a student but always have favourites and go home to masturbate over clothes stolen from the changing rooms.'

I stared at Tom, not knowing what to say. Why did he mention masturbating over clothes? Had he been spying on me? Watching videotapes of me? Was this situation more complicated than I imagined? Was it some sort of sting? And if not, why was he toying with me? Things had been tense between us since the argument at their house, but this didn't seem to be a good way of smoothing things over. I took a gulp of beer.

'But then along came Cherry,' he continued, 'and I don't agree with Judith. I don't think you have got low self-esteem. I think you've got very high standards. Or, rather, very specific standards. I'm uncertain how much of this story I believe ... I'm not saying you're lying, I just don't know what the truth is any more, and I'm not sure you do either.'

'All I care about is that she comes back to me.'

'And do you think that's going to happen?'

I shrugged. 'There seem to be two possible outcomes. One is that she comes back to me. The other is that sooner or later they phone me up and say that she's dead.'

'What do you think ... if anything ... will decide what happens?'

'My actions. I think this whole thing depends on me.'

Tom nodded and started to reply. I cut him off. 'Of course, even if they do say she's dead, it doesn't mean she really is. I think the most likely thing is that this probably was a sting, but then Cherry got cold feet, and now she's persuading them to let her return to me.'

'What about her illness?'

'I don't know. I'm assuming it's not as serious as it seems, but maybe I'm wrong. I do think it's real.'

He nodded, and placed his hand over mine. 'I think you're

right. But don't worry, I'm not like Judith, I do think your story will have a happy ending.'

Perhaps oddly, given the circumstances, his optimism made me relax. I think part of it was that I had just realised I could kill him.

But not tonight.

THIRTY-TWO

I didn't awake until ten-thirty the following morning. Tom and I had stayed up drinking until almost three; it had felt like a proper reconciliation. Most of the students had returned by the time we'd gone to bed, and a few of the bolder ones had stayed with us for a final drink before returning to their rooms. We hadn't agreed a time for assembling the following morning, although I'd assumed Tom would have got up for an early breakfast. But when I phoned his room, I woke him up.

'Sorry, Tom,' I apologised, 'I didn't realise you'd still be in bed.'

'It's OK,' he said, 'I knew I'd have to get up sooner or later. How's your head?'

'All right.'

'Really? Mine's terrible. Are you downstairs?'

I shook my head, which was silly, as he couldn't see me. 'No, I'm still in bed.'

He laughed. 'D'you think the students will have trashed Paris yet?'

'Well, it wouldn't be fun if we didn't have at least one trip to the police station. Do you want to go for breakfast, or should we track them down first?'

'Don't do anything yet. Let's meet in the lobby in fifteen minutes and go from there.'

'OK.' I put the phone down and got out of bed. I hadn't lied to Tom: my head did feel fine, even though I'd lost count of how many drinks we'd had last night. I had a quick shower, dressed, and took the primitive lift down to the ground floor.

Tom appeared ten minutes later. There were no students in reception.

'Seen anyone?' he asked.

'No.'

'OK,' he said, 'you're right, I'm being too uptight. They're probably having the time of their lives.'

We walked through the lobby. As we are going down the stairs to the street, Alison appeared.

'Hi, Alison,' said Tom. 'Everyone OK?'

She nodded. 'Yeah. Most are in a bar down the road. I don't know what it's called, but it has red walls and lots of bookcases.'

'OK,' he said. 'Where are you going?'

'I came back to look for you. What are we doing today? You said it was going to be busy.'

'Yes,' he said, 'and it will be. Just as soon as we've had our breakfast.'

It wasn't a busy day. The students seemed amused by our late start, and pleaded for a day on Parisian time. One small group, led by Frank Stone, a student I didn't know who was apparently a movie buff, headed off to watch a triple bill of American films that wouldn't be released in England for a few months at three different cinemas in and around Les Halles underground mall. I was tempted to join them, but worried that watching films would make me brood. Even trivial entertainment brings thoughts of death into my mind, and every time I go to the cinema the experience forces me to focus on the fact that I'm not going to be around forever. Instead, I took a group off to walk up Montmartre to the Sacré-Coeur while Tom took the others to the Pompidou Centre.

'You don't mind this, do you?' Tom asked just before we

set off. 'Tomorrow we can swap. You're getting the better deal really.'

I didn't understand why he thought I would mind until the students and I reached Montmartre. As far as I was concerned, all sightseeing was boring and I couldn't understand why he thought squinting at crappy modern art was the plum option. Then I realised it was the physical exertion he was avoiding and felt a flash of anger. Still, that was good. If those feelings kept coming tomorrow night would be a lot easier.

I persuaded the students to stop in so many cafés along the way that they started to get angry with me. But when we reached the Sacré-Coeur they soon tired of the mosaics and, apart from one black-clad girl fascinated by the notion that a relic of a piece of the sacred heart of Christ might be in the crypt, the students were as eager as I was to get back to the hotel.

When we returned, Tom and his group were already in the bar. He told us the film freaks were still at the cinema and suggested we should all go out for dinner together again this evening. Everyone seemed happy with this idea and I went upstairs to my room, pretending I needed another shower, but really craving some time away from the students. And from Tom.

Besides, I needed to practise. I had the knife hidden under my pillow, and thought I could remember all the moves Len had shown me, but I'd always been prone to stage fright, and knew that if Tom guessed what I was up to, even for a second, it would all be over.

THIRTY-THREE

The trip to the Pompidou Centre was less irritating than I'd imagined it would be. I wandered round the packed art-space with the Goth girl who'd been so impressed by the Sacré-Coeur, trying to guess which exhibits she'd like and which she wouldn't. She seemed pleased by the attention, and paused by a Kandinsky to ask me, 'Is Ms Smith really called Cherry?'

She was leaning forward, her back to the artwork, trying to see my face. Surprised, I said, 'Yes. Why?'

'It's such a cool name.'

'Really? I would've thought you'd hate it.'

'Why?'

'Isn't it too healthy? And all-American?'

'It's a cheerleader's name,' she said, smiling, 'and I love that punk-porno thing. Like Rose McGowan when she was going out with Marilyn Manson? I'm an artist myself, actually, and I've got this painting . . . the best thing I've done . . . called "My Perfect Date", and it's a self-portrait of me in a cheerleader outfit and pigtails giving a guy dressed up as a jock a blowjob in the alley next to a diner. It's like Edward Hopper meets Greg Dark. Or those captions in Kathy Acker's books, y'know, like the one in *Blood and Guts in High School* that says something like "Girls will do anything for love" with a graphic illustration of a woman's open vagina next to it.'

Usually, this sort of talk would have left me flustered, but I could tell Harriet wasn't flirting with me. She was obviously excited about her art, and pleased to get the opportunity to describe it. Oh, there was definitely an element of challenge in her explicitness, but it was the challenge of an artist who would be most impressed by an impassive response. And I liked the fact that she was pleased by Cherry's name. I felt an Adamic pride, happy someone had understood my choice. Her name did have all of those associations, and I had chosen it because I wanted to give this fantasy girlfriend a name I would feel guilty about every time I said it aloud.

'Shall we go and join the others?'

She smiled. 'OK.'

Back at the hotel we had an hour in the bar before Tom's group returned. My students looked smug, pleased they had got the irritating day out of the way first. Our film fans were still lost in action, improving their French by ordering snacks and buying tickets in the cinema. One of my group had told me they were at an all-day Macaulay Culkin retrospective, but I couldn't believe such things existed, even in France. So far we had got away with surprisingly little trouble from our students, and I knew Tom would be surprised when I put my plan into action in the early hours of tomorrow morning.

THIRTY-FOUR

I went to his room at three-thirty am. I had to knock on his door for almost two minutes before he shouted, 'I'm sleeping. This isn't funny. Leave me alone.'

'Tom,' I said, 'it's me. We've got a problem.'

'OK. Just let me put my trousers on.'

I waited until he opened the door, and then went inside with him.

'What is it?' he asked.

'One of the students just came back from a nightclub.'

'So? It's their last night. We told them they could go out.'

'No, it's not that. The student was scared. He said that Goth girl, what's her name?'

'Harriet.'

'Yeah, he said Harriet and a guy from our group, I don't know who, one of the ones who's been spending all his time in the cinema, have gone to this really heavy-duty S&M club and he's worried they've got themselves into something they're not going to be able to get out of, and they might get seriously hurt or violated.'

'It's a joke, Steve.'

'No. I don't think so.'

'Of course it is, they just want us to get caught in an S&M club. What's this place called? The Blue Oyster?'

'I don't know what it's called. But the student's given me a map.'

I held up a piece of paper with the directions I had copied

from *Force* magazine. Tom looked at it and said, 'Let me talk to this student.'

'He's gone to bed.'

'Steve, are you deliberately being gullible? Go and knock on his door.'

'I don't know which room is his.'

Tom stared at me for a minute, then sighed heavily and picked up his jacket. We left his room and took the lift down to the ground floor.

'What's wrong with you?' he asked. 'Why are you so nervous?'

'The student was really worked up. I'm scared about going into an S&M club, especially as I don't speak any French.'

Tom ignored me. 'Let me have another look at that map.'

I handed it over to him. He'd seen my handwriting several times before, but didn't seem to recognize it. If he did, I had an excuse ready, planning to tell him that I'd drawn the map from the student's instructions. But Tom just squinted at it and said, 'OK, this doesn't look too difficult.'

I'd been worried that a night porter might see us and get suspicious about two of us going out together and only one of us coming back, but there was no one in the lobby and the front door was open. We walked out into the street and Tom asked, 'Why on earth would they want to go to an S&M club anyway?'

'She's weird, that Goth girl. She told me this afternoon that she likes to paint pictures of herself giving blowjobs to strange men.'

'Christ, I hope she's not doing that now.'

'I don't think so. The student said they were doing something violent.'

Tom scowled. 'What is wrong with . . . ?'

'The youth of today?' I asked, smiling.

'When I was in the sixth form, I hadn't even had normal sex. Why is everything so fucking accelerated? What's Harriet going to get out of this experience?'

'Teenagers are curious, that's all. She's overage, and let's face it, it's got to be better than shagging M. Lafont.'

He looked angry. 'If you feel that way, why are we going to rescue them?'

'Because they don't know what they've got themselves into. I'm not defending them, I'm just saying we shouldn't be cross with them just because they're young. I mean, it's not that different from Jake and Lauren. They took my *parents* to an S&M club.'

Tom turned on me, suspicious. 'Why do you mention them?'

'I'm just saying . . . I thought you and Judith found that sort of thing cool.'

'Steve, Jake and Lauren are my friends. What they get up to in their personal life has got nothing to do with me . . . or you. They tell good stories, they're nice people, show respect to others, and know what they're doing. There's no connection between that friendship and this situation.'

I could tell Tom was exasperated. He stopped by the neon light of a shop window, puzzled over the map, and then led us down a different street.

'If all that S&M stuff started in France with the Marquis De Sade, why do they call flagellation *le vice anglais*?'

I waited for Tom to respond. This was my attempt to lighten the mood, which was silly and pointless, but for some stupid reason I didn't want him to be angry with me just before I killed him.

He ignored me. 'Are you sure it's down here?'

'It's the back entrance. See, look, on the map it says the doorway is just past those blue plastic dustbins.'

'OK,' he said, 'after you.'

'No, you go first.'

He looked at me, and then started slowly walking down the alleyway, one hand pressed against the wall.

I took out my knife.

THIRTY-FIVE

It took me an hour to get rid of Tom's clothes. I deposited them all over Paris, ending by throwing his tie into the Seine and giving his shoes to a tramp, a whimsical touch that could have proved fatal.

OK, I'm making light of it, but that seems to make more sense than ascribing any faux-grandeur to this tawdry moment. There was nothing noble about this murder. It was the physical reality of what I'd done that affected me, not the impact on my psyche. Intellectually, I had a sudden understanding that in spite of all my fears, once the memory of this moment had dulled, the fact that I'd broken the big commandment would worry me no more than breaking the little ones. But the *process* of killing someone, the interaction between us as I took Tom's life: that was what I found hard to handle. If it hadn't been for Len's training, his insistence on forgoing squeamishness and understanding this as a job that needed to be done, I would have fled after the first stab-wound. It took longer than I expected, longer than he had promised, and there was mess (although not as much as you might imagine, thanks to the precision Len had encouraged). But Tom knew what I was doing, it wasn't instantaneous, he cried and screamed and begged and said things to me, things I will never repeat to anyone.

The next thing I did, after it was over, was to go back out into the street to see if anyone had heard him. Satisfied that the world was continuing as normal – for everyone except

Tom – I returned to the alleyway and stripped the corpse, bundling his naked body into the first of the blue bins.

When I got back to the hotel, I went straight up to my room and got in the shower fully dressed. I stayed there until all my clothes were soaked, then got out, and hung them up around the room. Water from the clothes immediately started to soak the floor, but I didn't care. By the time they discovered any damage, I would be gone.

At breakfast the following morning, I took Alison aside and told her that Tom wouldn't be coming back with us because he had decided to stay in Paris a little longer and visit some friends. I'd assumed she'd swallow this explanation immediately, but she looked at me with an expression of extreme suspicion and said, 'Don't you need two teachers to supervise us?'

'Well, strictly speaking, yes, but you're a responsible group. He knows that won't be a problem. And if anyone else says anything, we'll pretend you're the teacher.'

Alison stared at me. I wanted to shout at her, but knew that would only make her less likely to believe me. She walked away and sat at a different table with some of the other students. I could tell she was telling them about Tom because they kept looking over at me and shaking their heads. I gave them my most serious glare, and drank my coffee.

Throughout the whole of the trip back, students kept coming up to me on the coach and asking me what had really happened to Mr Carson. It would have made me more paranoid if I hadn't realised that they all believed, and no doubt hoped, that it was some kind of sexual scandal that had detained their teacher. I suppose that, after Alison's misadventures with M. Lafont, this was an unsurprising assumption. I was also calm enough to realise that encouraging this sort of speculation would serve my alibi, and made sure that my replies to their questions had suitable ambiguity and the suggestion of sexual impropriety.

I visited Judith as soon as I got back. She took a while to answer the door, and when she did she seemed flustered, asking, 'Where's Tom?'

'Judith . . .' I started, about to launch into my false story. Before I had a chance, she said, 'It's her, isn't it?'

I didn't reply, wanting to know where she was going with this, and if her suspicions would be useful to me. She stood back to let me in and I followed her into the house. I noticed she was wearing grey and green gardening gloves.

'You know what the funny thing is, Steve? I always knew he would send you. For a man who considers himself brave, Tom is a terrible coward.'

I didn't know what to say. Judith sat down opposite me. She avoided my eye as she spoke, staring out of the window.

'Oh, you don't have to say anything. I'm not angry at you. It's not your fault. But you do know why he's sent you, don't you, Steve?'

I shook my head.

'It's because he knows I like you. He thinks . . .' She put a hand up to her eyes to stop the tears.

'I'm sorry,' I said.

'Don't,' she told me, 'don't apologise for him.'

This silenced me. I got up and walked over to Judith's chair, attempting to give her a hug. Her body felt stiff in my arms, and I realised what an incredibly awkward moment this was for her. But she seemed eager not to reject my kindness, and remained in this uncomfortable position until she said, in a different, calmer voice, 'Can you leave now, please? I really would prefer to be alone.'

I nodded and left her house, wondering where this left me.

PART EIGHT

THIRTY-SIX

They were waiting for me when I got back. It was the first time I'd seen Soumenda and Harry Hollingsworth together. Len was there too, opening a bottle of champagne.

'Congratulations,' said Harry Hollingsworth, 'you're ready for stage two.'

'There's nothing to celebrate,' I said sourly. 'You can put the champagne away.'

'Oh, come on, Steve,' said Harry, 'take pleasure where you can. Some of the most civilised nights that have ever occurred in the history of mankind have taken place in camps in the evening after a day on the battlefield.'

'He's a one, isn't he?' said Len, in admiration. I wasn't sure what guise he was currently in, and was waiting to hear if he was going to swear.

I ignored them and sat down. 'So, come on then, tell me, what's next?'

'It's only one more thing, Steve. Then it's all over and you can have Cherry back. She's doing really well, by the way, on the verge of a full recovery.'

'Can I see her?'

Harry shook his head, and looked disappointed in me. 'Not just yet, Steve. We don't want you to lose focus. Now, listen, we have to move fast. You did a good job with Tom, but we can't risk giving people time to get suspicious. This next stage is a bit more tricky, but shouldn't be quite so disturbing to you. Do you want to hear it now?'

I nodded.

'Do you understand what I mean by intimidation?' he asked, wiping his face with a red handkerchief.

'Of course. It's what you got Soumenda to do to me when I was in Cherry's mother's house.'

He laughed. 'Exactly right. Now I know what you're thinking and I have to disabuse you of the notion. I'm not in the *intimidation racket*, I'm a respectable businessman. I already told you that sometimes this business involves interaction in . . . international relations . . . but even at home intimidation can prove a necessary tool in even the most innocuous transactions. I don't get my hands dirty myself, that would be professional suicide, but Soumenda and some of my other employees take care of this for me.'

Soumenda looked absurdly proud, smirking and adjusting his tie.

'And one thing I've noticed, from their failures as much as their successes, is that women are much harder to intimidate than men.'

He stared at me, clearly wanting a response. I kept quiet.

'In answer to your question, I don't know why,' he continued, even though I hadn't said anything. 'I think it's because they don't like being told what to do. Most men are acutely aware of their position in the world. This means they're respectful to their superiors and when they get a reminder of who's in charge, they're scared enough to pay attention. But women, well, most women like a challenge. So intimidation tactics don't work on them. What it comes down to is that you have to provoke the right kind of fear. It's really difficult, but with someone you know it can be simpler because the complicity is already there. This probably doesn't make much sense to you. I'll get to the point. You know Mary, the geography teacher at your school?'

I nodded.

'Well, I'm sure you've noticed how close she is . . . was . . . to Tom?'

I didn't reply.

'Maybe you knew they were having an affair? It must have made you furious. You've become really fond of Judith, haven't you? It's sad. If you'd been a different sort of person, you could have had a wife like that.'

'I don't want Judith.'

'You want Cherry, I know, and don't worry – you're almost there. In fact, if you do this tonight, you can be reunited with her by morning.'

'Tonight?'

'It's best to get this over with quickly, Steve. It'll be easier for you to forget.'

'But I've been travelling all day, I'm exhausted.'

He smiled. 'All the better. We don't remember the things we do when we're tired, Steve. Tomorrow all this will seem like a bad dream. The final darkness before the happy ending.'

'What do I have to do?'

'I'll explain on the way.'

I had no choice. I followed the trio out to Harry's car. A silver BMW. I expected him to have a driver, but he climbed into that seat himself. Soumenda sat next to him, Len and I climbed into the back. The neighbourhood was quiet tonight. I watched a woman in a blue jacket putting an envelope into a post box. Len turned and grinned at me, beside himself with excitement. Harry drove slowly, handling his car with extreme caution. When we'd left my street, he seemed to relax and started talking again.

'It needn't be that unpleasant. You can even be truthful about the difficult situation you're in. Tell her you killed Tom, that'll get her attention. You don't have to be violent with her. All you need to do is scare her. Mary and Tom weren't just lovers, they also worked together, as a rogue unit. Now Tom's dead, Mary should be ready to retire, but there's always the possibility, the danger, that she might try to get in touch with ... people I don't want her to get in touch with. Again, I need you to trust me here, and accept that this is a matter of . . . well, I won't say national security, but near enough . . . and that I have reasons for instructing you in this way.'

'Harry's one of the good guys,' Len chipped in.

'Let me be precise. You have to tell Mary what you've done to Tom, make it obvious that you're prepared to do the same thing to her, and that the only way to prevent this unpleasantness is for her to keep quiet and to promise not to do anything about either avenging Tom's death or reinitiating contact with . . . Tom's friends. This operation shouldn't require any physical violence, but if it does work out that way, don't feel shy about roughing her up a bit.'

He let this sink in. I was filtering out all the talk of 'rogue units', and concentrating on what I needed to do to get Cherry back. We drove through the streets near my school, until he reached Mary's place. It was right on the outskirts of the danger area, just a few houses away from where the postcode changed and gentrification began. I had long harboured a desire to move into this area, and when my ceiling came down and I'd been saving my rent money for a deposit on a new place, it was here that I had in mind. Maybe when I got Cherry back we could move in here together, reward her for all the time she'd spent in my dusty hellhole. Harry's words repeated themselves: 'Some men can get used to anything. It's a sign of mental strength. But it can also be a weakness. If you're happy living in squalor, how are you ever going to aspire to luxury?'

'Will you need a weapon?' Harry asked me.

'No.'

'It's that door there.'

I walked up the front path. I rang the doorbell, praying she wasn't in. Within seconds, the door opened.

'Steve,' she said, surprised, 'what are you doing here?'

'Can I come in? It's important.'

Mary had the dazed expression that every teacher always

has when the day comes to an end. Her jet black hair was ruffled and she'd unbuttoned the top two buttons of her blue blouse. She looked at the car behind me. I turned and saw Len smiling and waving. He really was a buffoon. In spite of all my more pressing concerns, I couldn't help feeling embarrassed to be seen with him.

'OK,' she said.

I followed her through to the lounge. She picked up the remote and turned off the television. I sat down. She gestured to an open bottle of white wine.

'Like a drink?'

'No thanks.'

'So what is it?'

'I have something that I have to tell you. Someone has told me a story and I know that, whether that story is true or false, it's probably not going to affect the way that you respond. So before I tell you anything I need you to know that everything I've done I've done for love.'

She stared at me. I knew the only way to get through this was to tell her the whole story, as much to gear myself up for what I had to do as to provide her with an explanation.

'I'm sure Tom told you how Cherry came into my life. I met an old man in a bar and we got drunk together. Not long after, a man named Soumenda came to my house and asked me to fill out a questionnaire specifying what my perfect woman would be like. Then they told me that to get this perfect woman I had to work out where she was. They gave me an umbrella stolen from a hotel . . . I showed it to you in the staffroom that time, do you remember? The Tenderloin Hotel? Well, I went to that hotel and met Cherry and, as you know, she came to teach at our school. But then she got sick, really sick, and told me she thought she was dying. She refused to go to hospital, so I took her to her mother's house and then her mother phoned Soumenda, and she was taken away. They were going to make her better. But before they would make her better, they asked me to do two things for them. The first thing they asked me to do was kill Tom, which I did last night.'

Mary took a moment to respond to my words. Maybe she didn't believe me. I was a strange man; this could be a sick practical joke. But I kept a passive expression on my face, waiting for her to realise that I was telling the truth. When she did, she gulped, and then started crying.

'When I got back from France today, they were waiting for me in my house, and they told me that you were in league with the Fox, and that now you know that he's dead, you might be tempted either to seek revenge, or to get in contact with the Fox's people and offer your services in some way. They've sent me here to warn you that this would be a bad idea. This is all I have left to do, and then I will be reunited with the only woman I have ever loved. I realise you've lost someone close to you too . . . but I think he was bad for you and that you were probably misguided in following him. If you can give me your promise that you won't do anything stupid, then I can leave and nothing bad will happen.'

Mary continued to sob. I sat there, waiting while she composed herself. When she did, she picked up the telephone receiver next to her and said in a slow, patient voice, as if she was talking to a particularly stupid student, 'Steve, what I'm about to do now is phone the police. I don't want you to overreact. I understand what you've told me and I realise you've been manipulated by forces outside your control, but . . .'

'No,' I shrieked, jumping up, 'you mustn't. They're outside, they'll kill her . . . and you . . .'

I went to grab the phone. She jumped away, and then, with a careful, considered motion, punched me as hard as she could in the face. I felt my nose give in beneath her fist, and for some reason it felt like a relief. I struggled to get back up, looking for something to hurt her with as her fingernails clicked against the numberpads of her phone. She kicked me hard, and I went down, giving her enough time to connect to the emergency services and start to detail the situation in progress. I felt a blackness settle in behind my eyes as I picked up the wine bottle and moved towards her.

You know the rest . . .

THIRTY-SEVEN

Except that there is one last thing I haven't told you. I don't know whether I've been keeping it to myself because I was worried it would prejudice my case, or if it was just a secret I didn't want to share. But I did see Cherry one last time. She came to visit me: signed in under what will no doubt prove to be another alias. She was dressed completely differently and her hair was blonde, just as Len had said it was. The colour of her eyes had changed; even the shape of her eyebrows, now no longer plucked, was different. Was she admitting that it had all been a sham, that I'd been tricked? Maybe, but I'd prefer to see it like this. She'd changed because Cherry was dead, because Cherry was for me.

She sat with me for an hour without speaking. I don't know what she was trying to offer me, other than the knowledge she was still alive. Cherry was dead, but she was alive. It was comforting to know that I still loved her like this: the actress rather than the role. I remembered what she had told me on the morning she first went to the doctor about how if my specifications had been different I would have ended up with another ordinary executive from one of Harry Hollingsworth's many offices. And then I thought about the question Len had been trying to ask me when I found him in my flat: would I have committed murder for Cherry if she hadn't so completely fulfilled my fantasy?

I know you probably think it sounds strange (further evidence of delusion) that I didn't ask her to back up my story and confirm my alibi, such as it was. Especially as, of all the things you tried to get me to admit, the one that made me angriest was the suggestion that there was no Cherry; that I had killed Tom Carson and Mary because I was in love with Judith and couldn't bear the fact that my friend was betraying his wife with another woman.

But if you've come this far with me then you must realise that I had long since stopped caring about my sentence and worrying about whether you believed me. I was operating on a different level now, and because, above all else, I wanted my sacrifice to have meaning, all I could do was sit there holding her hands while she cried, repeating, 'It doesn't matter, it doesn't matter,' until the time was up and they took me back to my cell.

[S.E, 2005]

available from

THE ORION PUBLISHING GROUP

———————————

☐ **Tourist** £6.99
MATT THORNE
0 75381 137 5

☐ **Eight Minutes Idle** £6.99
MATT THORNE
0 75381 138 3

☐ **Dreaming of Strangers** £6.99
MATT THORNE
0 75381 132 4

☐ **Pictures of You** £6.99
MATT THORNE
0 75381 344 0

☐ **Child Star** £6.99
MATT THORNE
0 75381 753 5

☐ **Cherry** £6.99
MATT THORNE
0 75381 914 7

All Orion/Phoenix titles are available at your local bookshop or from the following address:

Mail Order Department
Littlehampton Book Services
FREEPOST BR535
Worthing, West Sussex, BNI3 3BR
telephone 01903 828503, *facsimile* 01903 828802
e-mail MailOrders@lbsltd.co.uk
(Please ensure that you include full postal address details)

Payment can be made either by credit/debit card (Visa, Mastercard, Access and Switch accepted) or by sending a £ Sterling cheque or postal order made payable to *Littlehampton Book Services*.
DO NOT SEND CASH OR CURRENCY.

Please add the following to cover postage and packing

UK and BFPO:
£1.50 for the first book, and 50p for each additional book to a maximum of £3.50

Overseas and Eire:
£2.50 for the first book plus £1.00 for the second book and 50p for each additional book ordered

---

BLOCK CAPITALS PLEASE

name of cardholder ....   *delivery address*
                                                             (if different from cardholder)
address of cardholder ....

....

....

        postcode ....   *postcode* ....

☐ I enclose my remittance for £......................................

☐ please debit my Mastercard/Visa/Access/Switch (delete as appropriate)

card number ☐☐☐☐☐☐☐☐☐☐☐☐☐☐☐☐☐☐

expiry date ☐☐☐☐   Switch issue no. ☐☐

signature ....

prices and availability are subject to change without notice